TRY TO REMEMBER ... VIETNAM

MIKE,
    HERE'S THE "JOHN NAM" BOOK.
HOPE YOU ENJOY IT.
                LOVE,
                JOHN

JULY - 2010

TRY TO REMEMBER ... VIETNAM

— JOHN R. HODGSON —

iUniverse, Inc.
New York   Bloomington

Try to Remember ... Vietnam

iUniverse books may be ordered through booksellers or by contacting:

iUniverse
1663 Liberty Drive
Bloomington, IN 47403
www.iuniverse.com
1-800-Authors (1-800-288-4677)

ISBN: 978-1-4502-3615-7 (sc)
ISBN: 978-1-4502-3617-1 (dj)
ISBN: 978-1-4502-3616-4 (ebk)

Printed in the United States of America

iUniverse rev. date: 06/07/2010

CHAPTER 1

Tyler Taylor sat at the back of the bus surveying the 40 or so men spread out in the seats in front of him. Maybe this is where I belong, he thought, the back of the bus. He definitely didn't want to be sitting up front. Whatever was coming, he was in no hurry to get there. Why he was going -- that he knew only too well. He closed his eyes and thought of his parents and their divorce and how that had plunged him into further depression. He however, didn't kid himself. He was well on the way to this trip right out of high school. He just didn't know it. What looked so promising then had all fallen apart by his sophomore year at USC. He had been kicked off the football team after numerous warnings from the coach. There was just so much he could overlook. His grades were dismal and without the football scholarship, he stopped going to class. By the end of the fall semester he received his draft notice. So much for being an architect, he thought.

"Hey man, do you think we'll end up in Nam?" The guy sitting next to Tyler asked as they drove further north towards Fort Ord.

Tyler had hardly noticed the short, boyish looking Mexican who was now staring at him. "Probably." Tyler replied. He didn't feel like talking.

"I signed up" the Mexican replied. "I want to be in the infantry and kill some Cong." Tyler just nodded. "Why do I have to sit next to the idiot on the bus?" he wondered. Looking around at the group traveling with him, he figured there were more.

Maybe he should have listened to his dad's advice about modeling himself after his best friend. Tim Rowe was in his sophomore year at Yale. He was the starting free safety on the football team and as usual getting good grades. Tyler had last seen him at Christmas break just after he had been kicked off the team. They had kind of drifted apart since then. Tim had a future; Tyler did too ... in the Army.

As the bus made its slow progress up the northern coast, Tyler looked out at the beautiful scenery of the Monterey Bay Peninsula. The long white beaches and groves of oak trees. He had looked up information about Fort Ord when he got his draft notice. It was over 28,000 acres and had been purchased by the Army in 1917 as an artillery range. Years before he had driven by it a couple times on trips to San Francisco with his parents. He just hadn't paid much attention to the Army base that would be home for the time being. The beauty of the area was lost to him after their arrival.

"All right, you Momma's boys, get your asses off the bus and line up in front of me."

Tyler moved off the bus and avoided eye contact with the drill instructor. Too much eye contact in the past usually resulted in a fight. Drinking and fighting had caused him to lose his scholarship. While he hated people at him, he had decided he would have to get used to it or end up in the brig. He took his place at the end of the quickly assembled line of men and placed his small athletic bag in front of him. It had the a USC graphic stenciled on the side. He had packed light, figuring the Army would give him what he needed. The DIs walked up and down the lines, stopping at times to harass some poor son-of-a-bitch. One stopped in front of Tyler and stared at his bag.

"What have we got here?" he asked, staring first at the bag, then at Tyler. "A big college boy. Were you at college, asshole?"

Tyler looked straight ahead and answered "Yes." The DI's eyes locked on Tyler's. "Yes what, asshole?" He roared.

"Yes, sir," answered Tyler.

"Yes, sir? Yes, sir?" screamed the DI into Tyler's face. "Do I look like I don't work for a living? Do I?"

Tyler's face flushed red. "No sir," he answered

"What is your name asshole?" The sergeant yelled.

"Private Taylor." Tyler yelled, staring directly into the DI's eyes.

"And you went to college, boy. What a sad commentary on our educational system," he yelled, walking a little up the line from Tyler. He then turned around ,ran back and got into Tyler's face again. "You will address me as sergeant. Have you got that, you college reject?"

Tyler had yet to even be sworn into the Army and was already losing his temper. When it came to "flight or fight", Tyler was always ready for the latter. This time, though, he bit his tongue.

"Yes, sergeant."

The DI stayed right in his face. "The rest of you worthless assholes will address us only when spoken to. Do you understand?"

"Yes, sergeant," the group replied in unison.

The sergeant walked slowly away from Tyler. "I'll remember you, Taylor", he said over his shoulder.

It wasn't what Tyler wanted, the asshole to remember him . The smart thing was to blend into the background and stay there.

Maybe in the next two years, Tyler thought, he would find out what it was that he wanted for the rest of his life. Either that or he wouldn't have to think about it. He thought about the television coverage he had started watching on the war. It wasn't pretty.

A flurry of activity followed. Tyler and the others got haircuts, were issued uniforms and assigned temporary housing for the night. He found himself staring at the ceiling from the top of the bunk he shared with a black kid from Watts. His name was Jimmy Johnson. Watts was only about 40 miles from Newport Beach; but it was a world away.

"Hey Taylor, what MOS are you looking to get into? Me, I want to be a military policeman. Instead of being pushed around by the pigs, I am going to be one," Johnson proclaimed from the bottom bunk.

The most knowledgeable of the new recruits had been talking about "MOS" – or military occupation specialty -- since their arrival on base. Tyler also discovered that nobody thought they would be in the infantry. Fat chance of that, thought Tyler.

"I don't know, Johnson. Maybe I'll apply for nuclear scientist or maybe a cook."

"What?" Johnson replied.

Tyler figured it didn't matter one way or another. The Army would put him where they wanted him. Right now he was freezing because all the windows were open in the barracks. One DI told them they were at risk of spinal meningitis, which evidently had spread throughout the base. So the windows would be open and once they reached their training barracks they would be restricted to it for their eight weeks of basic combat training. Great, thought Tyler, maybe I'll die of disease instead of being shot or blown up. After tossing around on the small bunk for a couple hours, he fell asleep.

CHAPTER 2

B-2-3. That was the name of his training barracks, lots of class -- a letter and a couple of numbers. No fancy names like the dorms Tyler had stayed in at USC. This was a drab gray building sitting on the top of a hill that overlooked a training field. A no frills hotel, he thought. There was a mess hall at the end of the long building. It looked like there were three or four sections that comprised the remainder of the building that groups of about 40 men stood in front of. He was in the first group of men who now moved into their new home.... If you could call it that.

Finally staying at the back of the line paid off. While the majority of guys were in one large barracks, the last six stragglers were assigned a separate room. He joined them. Most were draftees, but a couple were RA or regular army. After a while, those who had been drafted changed RA to mean real assholes. That came later, however. The first task was to unpack, make your bed the military way and fall out to the front of the barracks -- all in a couple minutes.

A DI stood in front of each of the four platoons that made up the company. At the top of steps, overlooking the company, stood a single DI. He surveyed the men who stood at attention below his gaze. He waited a full minute before speaking.

"Men, my name is Sergeant Crooker and you'd better remember that."

Crooker began walking in front of each platoon, surveying the men who were standing at attention. Tyler managed a quick glimpse at the DI standing in front of his platoon. He looked hard and in very good shape, thought Tyler. He had the look of his old linebacker coach at USC. The sergeant strutted toward the next platoon. His booming voice could be heard from the end of the farthest formation. If a bulldog could talk, this is what he would sound like, Tyler thought.

"You will listen and react to every order you are given by your drill instructor and any other cadre you may come in contact with. Is that understood?"

The company answered in unison, a resounding "Yes, sergeant."

Crooker, who had turned his back to the company spun around quickly with a look of disgust on his face.

"What did you pussies say? I can't hear you. Do you have any balls?"

Again the company tried to appease the square-jawed sergeant. "Yes, sergeant," they all screamed.

Tyler was getting bored by the psychological play. He knew the harassment was going to feel like hell week in football, except this lasted eight weeks. He moaned silently. At least the physical training wouldn't be too bad. He had stayed in shape after football ended in spite of all the partying and drinking. He was 6 foot 2, weighed 220 pounds and had been lifting weights since high school. Most of the guys around him looked out of shape. Crooker walked away into the barracks. The DI who was standing in front of his assigned platoon turned to address them.

"I am Sergeant Merelli and I will lead you for the next eight weeks of training. At the end of your training we will be the best platoon in this company. Is that understood?"

"Yes, Sergeant!" the men replied, almost in unison.

Merelli paced the front line, eyeing every soldier as he walked by.

All of a sudden he ran up to an unlucky draftee in the second row and read the soldier's name at the top of his breast pocket . "Patterson, what is a retard like you doing in this man's army? Why isn't your shirt tucked in?

Patterson said nothing, probably not sure of which question to answer first, Tyler thought.

"Drop down and give me 20 push-ups." Merelli yelled. Patterson fell to the ground and started doing his push-ups.

"You will count them out as you do them Private Patterson. Start over."

As Patterson yelled out the numbers of his punishment, Merelli continued walking among the soldiers, who desperately tried to avoid looking him in the eye. Tyler thought he looked pretty wimpy for a drill instructor. Unlike Crooker, Merelli was short, maybe 5 foot 7, and maybe weighed 150 pounds soaking wet. He had a hawkish nose, short black hair and wore thick black plastic glasses with coke bottle lenses. He must have evidently let a smile creep onto his lips, because Merelli suddenly turned and barked at him.

"Do you think this is funny Private Taylor?"

Tyler looked straight ahead over the DI's hat. He still had a little smirk on his face. "No, Sergeant. I am just a happy person." Tyler said sarcastically. What the hell, he thought, might as well have some fun.

"Is that right, Taylor?" Merelli said, looking at some of the other recruits.

"Anybody else happy here?" When no one answered, Merelli again addressed Tyler.

"Well Taylor you may be the only happy son-of-a-bitch in this platoon and that makes me sad. Private Taylor, you can return to the barracks. The rest of you unhappy assholes drop and give me 50."

Taylor stood there at first staring at the sergeant. "I told you to get out of here wiseass. Now move." Merelli barked at him.

Tyler ran back to the barracks thinking that he had managed to get attention he didn't want. He also thought- I can kick this guy's ass.

Ten minutes later the rest of his platoon returned to the barracks on the run. One of them yelled at him.

"Hey Taylor, Merelli is inspecting the barracks in five minutes."

The rest of his roommates ran in and started putting away their equipment and clothing. Tyler jumped up from his bunk and tried to neatly store his stuff. He didn't need to be noticed again.

CHAPTER 3

What the hell am I doing here? Tyler was at the back of his platoon, pushing an overweight recruit along as they jogged out to the rifle range at Fort Ord. The guy, whom Tyler didn't really know very well, was having a very bad time trying to keep up. Sgt. Merelli's idea of fun was to turn around the whole platoon and double back to pick up the stragglers so he had decided to help out.

"What's the matter, Harwood, did you drink too much beer at college this last semester?" Merelli yelled at the guy Tyler was pushing.

"Harwood, you miserable fuck, you carry your own rifle," he screamed after noticing that Tyler was carrying both his and Harwood's M-14s. "Never put down your rifle. Do you hear me?" Merelli was now running along beside Harwood as Tyler continued to push him from behind.

"Give him his rifle Taylor." Merelli yelled at Tyler.

Harwood evidently got scared and picked up the pace on his own. As Merelli continued to berate him about being fat and out of shape, Harwood moved towards Tyler for his rifle. As he reached for it, he tripped and stumbled to the ground. Tyler was able to jump over the fallen soldier as the rifle fell to the ground. He looked back in time to see Harwood vomit on Merelli's highly polished boots. Tyler smirked, but knew this would not be good for any of them.

"Platoon, halt."

Merelli barked out the order just as the platoon neared a rifle range along the beach. Tyler glanced back to see Merelli pull the 250 pound Harwood across the vomit that covered his boots. Tyler was impressed with the strength of the skinny DI.

"Platoon, attention! About face." Merelli yelled at the men, who turned to face him almost in unison, except for the fallen Harwood, who had made no move to stand.

"What we have here people is an out of shape puke who in combat will get you killed. Why you might ask? Because you have to wait for him, you have to care for him and his equipment instead of caring for yourself and your mission. But you know what? The U.S. Army doesn't leave people behind. So you get to carry him."

Merelli assigned two other guys to carry Harwood . Tyler joined his squad and they marched to the rifle range. Tyler looked out at what was the beauty of the Fort Ord coastline, the ice plant was blooming in the sand, gulls were flying overhead and he could smell the ocean. From where they were he could barely see the shoreline and wondered if the surfing was any good here. Right now it looked flat, but he would still love to be in the water.

For some reason he started thinking of Patty Olsen. She had been his girlfriend and surfing companion in high school. Since then she had become another causality of poor decisions he had made. She frequently crept into his thoughts unexpectedly. She was married now and belonged to someone else. He hadn't seen her since his freshman year of college, but he knew she would always be buried in his heart. Patty Olsen, except it wasn't Olsen anymore. Now it was Bedford. She had married a guy named Sam Bedford who she had met at Orange Coast Community College after their final breakup. She was the only girlfriend he had who really understood him, but their romance just seemed to evaporate when he went to USC. He barely saw her with football, studies and all the parties. He didn't even blame her when she finally called to tell him it was over. At the time it didn't seem to matter.

He was having a ball, even if he wasn't starting for the Trojans yet. He had been recruited by John McKay at the end of his senior year at Newport Beach High. His team had won the 3A California Interscholastic Federation's championship and he had made first team All-CIF at linebacker. There were plenty of girls at SC for him. It wasn't until things starting going bad that he thought about losing her.

Your mind and heart are funny things he thought. One, you can occasionally lie to and get away with it. The other just won't let you forget when you fuck up. He realized that thinking about the ocean had opened the door to thoughts of Patty. She started out as his surfing buddy. Patty was the only girl in high school who could keep up with the guys and most of the time-she could show them how it was done. She was a jock, but a very cute one. While they dated on occasion during his sophomore and junior year, it wasn't until their senior year when they really got serious.

They had never had sex until then. But as soon as they did, she became very obsessive about their relationship and talked about marriage all the time. He couldn't understand it. He knew that to get anywhere in the world he needed an education. But she was hardly interested in junior college let alone USC. He had suggested she go there with him. She wasn't interested and for whatever reason, wanted out of her parent's home. Tyler could never figure out why, except her father seemed very possessive. So she went from a very nice beach home to living in Santa Ana on Sam's grocery checker wages. He had kept up on the rumors from Tami Hillman; she had been Patty's best friend in high school and still stayed in touch with them both.

His thoughts were interrupted by Sgt. Merelli's cadence song. "Jody was there when you left."

"Your right" was the response and you hoped your right foot was just touching the ground. Jody... was the mythical guy who was not only fucking your wife or girlfriend, but your sister too, while you were off dying for your country. Real morale boosting song, Tyler thought. Sam was there when he left. Unfortunately he had every right to be.

CHAPTER 4

In the third week of basic they had the first physical fitness test. It consisted of a mile run, a grenade toss and other forms of torture intended to determine your overall fitness. Tyler easily completed the run in just five minutes, even with combat boots on. He was in the first group to finish and they stood off to the side watching the stragglers.

"Hey, Taylor, wouldn't you hate to flunk and recycle all this crap?"

Tyler looked over at his platoon leader.

"Yeah, that would be fun." Tyler replied.

According to Sgt. Merelli if a recruit didn't pass the physical at the end of basic, he had to repeat it. It was called a recycle. At least a third of his company hadn't passed today, and he was sure this would mean a lot more training in the remaining five weeks of basic.

He wondered what type of advanced training he would be assigned. He had taken a battery of intelligence tests the first week they were here. He was interviewed and encouraged to apply for Officers Candidate School or OCS. The sergeant who talked to him said with his scores, he was wasting his time as an enlisted man. The interview was followed up with a group meeting of the other trainees who qualified for OCS.

A young second lieutenant with a baby face ran down all the virtues of being an officer. Tyler had read that in combat, they were usually the first guys killed. Besides he only wanted to do his two years and get out. After declining OCS, he was asked what training he was interested in. When he said the infantry, the sergeant almost fainted.

"That's where the dumb asses are sent, Taylor. Them and cooks. Do you want to be with them?"

The truth was he really didn't care what they did with him. He was paying his penance for all those past sins. He didn't tell the sergeant that. He just shrugged his shoulders.

"OK, Taylor, they could use a couple smart guys like you in the infantry. What I put down still doesn't mean you will get it. That's the Army way you know."

That night at dinner Tyler sat down across from a guy he had pegged as maybe being more off plumb than he was. His name was John Raab and he already had a reputation for pushing the DI's. The guy ran like a deer and never seemed to get tired. He was thin but muscular. He had sharp, angular features and wore old fashioned wire rimmed glasses that he was constantly pushing up on his nose. He had perfectly straight white teeth and seemed to be smiling all the time at some private joke only he knew.

"John, right, I am Tyler Taylor," Tyler said, extending his hand to Raab.

"My friends usually just call me Raab," he said, shaking Tyler's hand.

"So where are you from, Raab?" Tyler asked, inspecting a plate that he suspected held a pork chop.

"The beautiful city of Burbank. How about you Tyler?"

"Newport Beach." Tyler said now trying what he thought were mashed potatoes.

"Oh, one of those surfers who forgot there was a war going on, with a draft," Raab said, looking directly into Tyler's eyes.

"Yeah, something like that," Tyler said, shaking his head.

There was something about Raab that Tyler immediately liked. That was unusual for him. He didn't make friends easily.

They continued talking after returning to the barracks. Raab, like Tyler, had been in college when he was drafted. Unlike Tyler he hadn't been kicked out of school. He had graduated from Loyola University and was considering grad school when he got his notice.

"I figured everyone else I knew was going, so what the hell, might as well get it over with. I just didn't think it would be this quick." Raab explained to Tyler.

They talked until the lights were turned off for the night and Raab made his way back to his bunk in the main barracks.

Tyler woke up in early morning darkness. He had been dreaming about his mother. It was funny; she was only a couple miles from here, in Big Sur. She had left her nursing career in Newport Beach and joined a commune of artists, all of them trying to find themselves. He personally thought she sucked as an artist. She had a boyfriend 10 years younger. Some wild-eyed hippie, he imagined, but he had yet to meet him. He wasn't sure when he would see his mother again. She had pretty much destroyed his father when she left. He had to sell the beach house on 42nd Street and now lived a couple blocks off the beach in a much smaller, older home. His dad had given her half their assets and Tyler envisioned her supporting the boyfriend and whoever else befriended her. She would probably be broke in a couple years, he thought. He wondered if he would ever forgive her . His thoughts were interrupted by Sergeant Merelli entering his room and turning on the lights and at the same time yelling for everyone to get up. He looked surprised to see Tyler standing by the window looking out at the creeping fog that blanketed the hill.

"What's the matter, Private Taylor, having trouble sleeping? Maybe we're not working you hard enough."

"No, Sergeant. I was just meditating before starting another glorious day in this man's Army," Tyler replied, standing rigidly at the window.

"Well meditate this, Taylor: Get your ass dressed and fall out in 15 minutes."

Merelli left the room and continued through the barracks, turning on more lights while cursing surprised recruits. Tyler made his up his bunk, dressed and stood outside waiting for the stragglers when Raab showed up and stood next to him.

"Tonight I am going to take care of Merelli. That little Italian needs a tune up, don't you think Tyler?" Raab gave Tyler a wink.

As Tyler had suspected, the day involved a lot of physical training, or PT for short. The Army had an acronym for everything. As they went through a series of calisthenics, he realized that even with all the football and surfing he had done that this was the best shape he had ever been in. He figured he had lost about 10 pounds in the last couple weeks. All the pull-ups and push-ups had added muscle to his arms. He had to admit he felt pretty good in spite of the constant harassment from the DIs. The long day ended with another long run around the training compound. It was early evening before they were dismissed.

That night, as he and Raab sat in the main barracks discussing the lives they had left behind, Merelli's voice came over the intercom.

"You men are too loud. Keep it down!"

Raab immediately hit the button on the speaker. "Come down and make us, you little Wop."

Raab grinned at Tyler as they heard Merelli running down the corridor towards the barracks. Merelli ran in looking around at a bunch of mostly scared recruits.

"Which one of you miserable assholes had the balls to say that? Or do you all want take another run tonight instead of sleeping?"

The assembled men let out a collective moan. Before anyone said anything Raab stood up.

"I guess you got me, Sergeant. It was me", Raab answered, looking straight into Merelli' s eyes.

Tyler thought for once Merelli didn't look as confident as usual, but only for a few brief seconds. "OK, wise guy, we're going for a little night run," he said, hustling Raab out of the barracks. Tyler looked out the window and saw them run off into the night.

He didn't see Raab until the next morning . He woke, as the lights were turned on, to find him just entering the barracks. "I don't think Sergeant Merelli will be joining us today," Raab said ,leaning against Tyler's bunk with a big grin on his face.

Tyler jumped out of the bed and stared at his new friend.

"So what happened?" he asked eagerly.

Well," Raab said, flashing a crooked smile.. "We ran out towards the rifle range for about 10 miles. The sergeant stayed up with me until we made the turn to come back. The last thing I heard was him yelling at me to come back. I think he's still out there."

Raab may have been right. They didn't see Sergeant Merelli for the rest of the day. They had a substitute DI, who said nothing about Merelli's absence. Raab by far was one of the strangest people Tyler had ever met. He would make a great friend.

CHAPTER 5

It wasn't until the sixth week of basic that Tyler finally got to drink a beer. He found it odd that he really hadn't thought about drinking prior to that. All the troubles it had caused him in college and here the Army had him cold turkey in six weeks. His squad was allowed to buy two cans at the Post Exchange and any sundry items they needed. They drank the beer outside -- very quickly.

"So, Tyler, what did you sign up for?" Raab asked as he chugged a Coke down. He didn't drink any alcohol Tyler had learned.

"Infantry," Tyler shrugged. He had learned just how unpopular that answer was in the last six weeks.

Raab only nodded.

"What about you?" Tyler asked.

"Well, I heard from one of the cadre that medics don't have to do KP, so I signed up for that. I hate KP." KP, or kitchen patrol, as Tyler had learned, consisted of waking at 3 in the morning and then cleaning up after the three meals of the day. He got to scrub pots and pans on his one assignment there so far. He had decided that one of the personality traits the Army must look for in cooks was sadism. What a bunch of assholes, he thought.

He was half-way through his second can of beer when Merelli exited the PX. "You have about 30 seconds to finish those beers," Merelli shouted at the group gathered at the end of the building.

Tyler tossed the remainder of his last can in the nearby trash can. He realized under the circumstances it didn't taste all that great. He was glad he did as Merelli made them double time back to the barracks. One of the guys puked after running the mile back. The Army, he thought, could ruin just about anything that gave you pleasure.

The next couple of weeks were more of the same, with the exception of the gas chamber, when they were marched out to a cinder block building and handed gas masks.

"Men, you will enter the building with your gas masks on," Merelli said. "There is tear gas vapor inside and you will hold on to the shoulder of the man in front of you as you circle the room. If you don't hold on you will not be able to see, as the gas is very thick. After we demonstrate the effectiveness of your gas mask, you will be required to remove it and continue walking around the room until you are led outside," Merelli said, with just a hint of a grin.

Tyler entered the room holding onto Raab's shoulder. Merelli was right. It was hard to see -- especially after they pumped in more tear gas. He thought he was feeling a little of the gas through his mask when, after circumnavigating the room twice, they were ordered to stop.

"Who thinks they can feel the effects of the gas?" Merelli yelled through his gas mask. Several hands went up, but Tyler decided not to raise his. He was learning never to volunteer anything.

"So you think you feel the gas, Henderson?" Merelli said to a recruit in front of Tyler.

"Take off your mask, Henderson."

Henderson removed his mask and immediately started coughing, his face turning bright red as he struggled to breathe. "OK, the rest of you, take off your masks and start walking."

The gas hit Tyler immediately. He tried to breathe as shallow as he could, but the gas was burning his eyes and he coughed hard trying to rid his lungs of the noxious gas.

After circling the building once, they were allowed to go outside. Snot ran from his nose as he exited the building.

The worst was yet to come; he just didn't realize it yet.

Merelli gave them about 10 minutes to recover.

"All right, you've completed the easy part," he said. "You will now navigate your asses through the obstacle course. You will crawl through the field in front of you where you will encounter CS gas at some point. You will then remove your gas mask from the holder, place it on your face and complete the course."

Merelli marched them over to the field. Tyler looked out at a 50 yard course that had concertina wire strung across it in a half a dozen places. There were trenches below the wire that you had to wriggle through without getting caught on the barbs.

"You will not reach for your gas mask until you are exposed to the gas," Merelli warned. "If you do, you will start the course over again."

Tyler was in the middle of the formation when the order was given to move out. He had just crossed the first strand of wire when he saw one of the sergeants spraying gas along the trench he was in. The gas hit him as he reached for his mask. It was overwhelming. Just as he got the mask on, he had to puke. He slipped the mask off his chin and vomited off to the side. He replaced the mask and started crawling. He heard some commotion off to his right and saw one soldier get up and start running back to the rear where the DIs were standing. He could hear them yelling at the man who looked like he had gone crazy. Tyler finished the course and looked back to see the hapless soldier trying to fight three rugged DIs. He had never seen anyone look so frightened. Raab moved over next to him, he gave Tyler one of his crooked smiles.

"So what do you think, Tyler? CS, it must stand for chicken shit, huh? "

Tyler wasn't sure, but he never wanted to breathe CS gas again. Of that he was sure.

CHAPTER 6

Tyler learned one thing the last week of Basic. The Army wasn't kidding when they said you would repeat if you didn't pass the last test. Six sad soldiers carried their gear into his room and reluctantly stored it. This was their new barracks. He looked over at Cornwall, who was staring out the window, holding back tears. He was a giant of a man who most of the guys called "Baby Huey." Tyler actually felt sorry for him. He probably should have never been allowed into the Army. He must have weighed at least 350 pounds when they started Basic. He had lost a lot of it, but he was still overweight and out of shape. Tyler figured he might spend his whole enlistment in Basic.

Tyler grabbed his duffel bag and exited B-2-3 for the last time. Earlier, he had received his orders for advanced training and marched in the graduation parade. He was going to be a 91A10, a medical corpsman. He didn't get infantry after all. Raab got the same orders. They would train together. Everyone said the medical training was at Fort Sam Houston in Texas, but for some reason they had orders for Fort Riley, Kansas. He would have preferred Texas over Kansas, but he had never seen either. The only medicine he knew about was the first aid course he had taken back in the Boy Scouts. Guess he would learn.

He had debated his next move for the last eight weeks. Should he stop and see his mother in Big Sur. He didn't decide until he arrived at the bus station and purchased the ticket. He called his dad and told him he was going to see her and would be a day late getting home to Newport Beach.

He decided not to call her. He caught a bus in Seaside and got off at the Big Sur Inn, the scenery spectacular as always. . He checked at the desk and got directions to the art colony. He hitched a ride and within an hour he was standing outside the gates of her new world.

They evidently weren't used to seeing a soldier in uniform standing outside their gate, his duffel bag slung over his shoulder. A middle-aged man met him as he entered the compound. He had long thinning hair and a full beard. He wore torn jeans and a "Grateful Dead" t-shirt. He smelled of marijuana and patchouli oil.

"Can I help you, friend?" the man tentatively asked with a welcoming smile.

Tyler set down his bag and stared at his welcoming committee. The bearded hippie had been joined by two younger men both wearing psychedelic t-shirt and beads. All three had very long hair.

"I am looking for Jill Taylor." Tyler said, gazing at the small cottages he could see in the distance.

"What do you want with Jill, soldier?" the older hippie inquired.

"Just tell her that Tyler is here."

One of the younger hippies ran off. It was evident to Tyler that he was peacefully being blocked from entering any further.

Soon he saw his mother running towards him. She was wearing jeans and a peasant blouse and had no bra on. Her hair was pulled back in a pony tail and she wore no make-up. He couldn't help but marvel that she was still slim and shapely and looked a decade younger than her 42 years. She had tears in her eyes as she hugged him hard.

"Oh Tyler, I can't believe you're here. Look at you, you're a soldier," she said, touching his short cropped hair. "Come on, I want you to see my cottage."

Tyler picked up his bag and walked past the welcoming delegation. He followed his mother back into a wooded area, where a small two bedroom cottage sat like a prop from a Disney movie. Inside there were numerous canvases on easels. He recognized his mother's work, but saw a different style on some of the paintings. He was just going to ask her who the other artist was when a guy about 30 years old emerged from the back bedroom. He had a light brown beard, long hair and a slim build. He extended his hand towards Tyler.

"Hi, brother. I am Danny, your Mom's friend."

Tyler shook his hand, with as much pressure as he could exert. So this is the boyfriend he thought; a boy not much older than himself. He was instantly disgusted with his mom and the piece of shit holding onto his hand. His mother was beaming like some junior high school cheerleader.

Danny quickly released his hand from Tyler's grip. So this was who his mom had given up her marriage vows to his father. A skinny hippie with probably no future. He released an audible sigh as he looked at the man.

"Let's sit down and talk, honey." His mother motioned towards a small wooden table in a very small kitchen.

"Danny, get us some wine. This is a celebration!" His mom took out some cheese from a small refrigerator and cut it up while Danny poured them each a glass.

Tyler found it hard to talk as he contemplated his mother's new boyfriend. He looked so young, but so did she...

He gave her a very brief rundown on Basic Training.

"I am going to be trained as a medic, mom." Tyler said as he sipped his wine. It was good.

His mother looked concerned. "Will you have to go to Vietnam?" she asked.

"I don't know yet, but probably."

Tyler looked down into the dark liquid. Danny pulled a joint out of his pocket. "Want to do a little weed, Tyler?"

Tyler looked up from his drink. "I just do the liquid stuff, Danny," he said, with a little too much sarcasm. His mother caught it immediately.

"Danny, why don't you do that later? Maybe you could give Tyler and me a little time alone." Danny stuffed the joint back in his shirt pocket and smiled at his mom.

"Sure, Hon. I need to hit the Post Office anyway."

After he left Tyler poured himself another glass of wine.

"Are you sure this is what you want, Mom? You know dad still loves you. He's miserable without you."

It was his mom's turn to look down at her wine.

"I know this is hard on you Tyler, but I am done with your father. He could never understand this lifestyle."

"Well, who in the hell could understand this hippie shit?" He glared at his mother.

"What have you become, Mom, some dope smoking radical hiding out in Big Sur? I was surprised the guys at the gate didn't have guns."

"Oh, Tyler, this place is all about peace and love. I am just sorry you can't see that."

Tyler got up from the table and quickly downed his drink.

"Thanks for the wine," he said, walking out of the cottage with his mother following him.

"Tyler, please don't leave. Let's talk," she said, holding onto his sleeve.

"I can't handle this place and it doesn't seem like we have a lot to talk about. I'm not interested in being here when your boyfriend returns. If you do want to get in touch with me you can call me at the house. I have leave for a couple of weeks."

He never looked back as he left the compound. He didn't belong there. He knew that for sure.

The bus ride to Newport Beach gave him time to think, maybe too much. In addition to his mother, he was thinking about Patty again. He daydreamed about calling her. Just as an old friend saying "Hi." Who was he kidding? She would know it was more than that. Forget her; he told himself, she was married. He tried to sleep, but he kept thinking about the last time they had made love -- or was it lust? He had come home for the weekend. His dad had gone sailing with friends and he had picked Patty up at her house. It was just after football season had ended. He had sat on the bench all year, but he still thought he was pretty hot. He had talked her into going back to his house. He wasn't tender in his love making. She was crying after they finished.

"You don't love me, Tyler. You just use me," she said. "You're not the same anymore. You're just a jock with a big head. Please take me home." She looked at him with pleading eyes.

That night she called and told him it was over. She just didn't feel the same about him. More importantly she was sure he didn't feel the same about her.

"You know, Tyler, some day this will all catch up with you. I feel sorry for you."

It was the last thing she had said to him. At the time he didn't care. Now he did. He wasn't a big college football player anymore. He was a private in the U.S. Army.

It was hot when he arrived at the beach; not like those cold nights at Fort Ord. After dinner with his dad, he went to bed and slept for 12 hours. He woke early the next morning and walked down to the beach with his board. He hadn't been in the water for nine weeks and it was the first thing he wanted to do. He had two weeks before he had to report to Fort Riley. He was going to make the best of it.

The waves were mostly flat and well spaced. Tyler didn't care. He just took in the smell of the ocean, the swell of the waves, the gray/blue water and the beauty of the Newport Coast. He was back in his element and he smiled broadly for the first time in awhile.

A couple hours in the water and he felt like a new man. After a shower and quick breakfast, he headed for the garage to pull out his old '46 Ford 'Woody' that he and his father had rebuilt when he was in high school. The wagon was still in great shape and Tyler couldn't imagine selling it. His dad had promised he would keep it in the garage, even though it meant his car would have to be parked on the street. It was a hassle this time of the year, with all the tourists in town for summer vacation competing for parking. He thought about his dad; what a good guy he was. He wondered if he would ever get over his mom leaving. Tyler knew his dad still loved her.

He pulled out onto Balboa Boulevard and headed out to Pacific Coast Highway. He turned south toward Corona Del Mar to surprise his old friend Tim Rowe. Tim was completing his sophomore year at Yale and was home for spring break. They had only exchanged one letter while he was in Basic. What was he going to say? "Love the Army?"

He pulled up to the gate outside the Rowe compound. Tyler easily remembered the code and punched it on the keypad. Tim's' 62 Corvette was parked out front with the top off. Tyler knew that Tim had not taken the car back East. He was afraid the harsh winter and lack of a garage would damage his beloved Vette. Instead, he had purchased a used VW beetle to get him around New Haven. Tyler just shook his head at the contrast. He parked the 'Woody' behind the Vette and walked to the front door just as Tim bounded out of it.

"Holy shit, you're back!" Tim ran up and hugged him.

He had a million questions about the Army and Tyler barely could answer them when Tim had another one.

"So what about Vietnam? Do you think you'll have to go?" Tim finally got to the big question after they had each grabbed a beer and sat out by the pool.

"I don't know yet. You won't believe this, Tim, but I am going to be a medic. Me, who hates the sight of blood!" Tyler finished the cold beer and got up to retrieve another from the cooler.

He explained the training he was to receive in Kansas. Tim took it in still sipping on his first beer.

"We've been talking a lot about the war at school Tyler. A lot of the students think it's immoral. I am pretty sure I don't want to go." Tim said in a serious tone.

"Tim, it's all that liberal crap you get at Yale. Anyway I am not going right at this moment and we have some serious partying to do before I head out to boring Kansas."

Tyler downed his second can of beer for emphasis.

Tim wasn't quite ready to drop the subject yet.

"I hear being a medic is really dangerous. The Viet Cong supposedly target them."

Tyler just shrugged his shoulder. "Maybe Tim. I guess I'll find out if I go."

"And another thing," Tim was not giving up, Tyler thought. "Why were you really kicked off the team? What happen with school?"

Tyler gave a cold stare at his friend. "Let's talk about it later, Tim." Tim nodded in agreement. He knew Tyler would answer the question in his own time.

"So what girls are in town? Have you seen anyone we would like to see?" Tyler said, quickly changing the subject. Tim explained he had only been home a couple of days and really hadn't been out much. He had worked part time at his dad's law office. As usual his dad wanted him to consider law school after he graduated. Maybe he would and keep his student deferment and avoid the draft.

"I met a guy in Basic I think you would like Tim. His name is John Raab. I invited him down here this week. He can be our chauffeur, he doesn't drink. He'll be here in a couple days. Can you believe he lives in Burbank and has hardly even been to the ocean?"

"He doesn't drink and doesn't surf and you're friends with him? I've got to meet this guy." Tim just shook his head and wondered who this guy Raab was. Tyler didn't make friends very easily and he so far hadn't heard a thing they had in common.

Tyler still wanted to talk about partying. "So where can you dance now that the Rendezvous burned down?"

The Rendezvous had been a popular ballroom since the '20s. They had spent a lot of time there during high school. Its beachside location would be missed.

"They still hold dances at Harmony Park, but I hear it's getting kind of rough. There are some good bars down by the Island, near coast highway. Lots of young college girls now that UC Irvine opened. At least that's what I hear," Tim said, belching from the beer.

"You want to give it a try tonight?" Tyler asked.

"Sure, even if you do look like an Army poster." Tim had been fixated on Tyler's buzz cut. "I am sure some hard up girl will take pity on you."

It only took a second for Tyler to react. He shook his beer and sprayed it all over his friend. Tim laughed and jumped into the pool.

"We'll see how you do tonight, now that you're a trained killer."

CHAPTER 7

Tyler woke up with a fright. He didn't know where he was, but it appeared to be a bathroom floor. He knew this because he was hugging the toilet. The cool Spanish tile felt good against his aching head. He could hear a whirling sound and wondered at first if it was also in his head. When he finally looked up, he could see that the bathroom light and fan were both on. Looking around he realized he was in the Rowe's pool side cabana. When they were in high school, this was where their live-in housekeeper Lupe lived. She still worked for the Rowe's, but now she had her own place since getting married. He pulled himself up to the sink and splashed water on his face. He still had no recollection of how he got here or what happen last night after he and Tim went bar hopping. At least he remembered Tim was driving. This was the same way he felt the morning of his dismissal from the USC football team. He couldn't remember that morning what had taken place the night before either. He learned all about it from Coach McKay. After searching the bathroom cabinets, he found a new toothbrush, toothpaste, shaving crème and a razor. Just what he would expect from Mrs. Rowe he thought, stepping into the shower.

He felt a little better after cleaning up, with the exception of having to put back on the clothes from the night before. Tim was eating breakfast beside the pool when he came out. Lupe ran up to him.

"Mr. Tim, would you like some breakfast too?"

"Just coffee and orange juice, Lupe." She walked off towards the house. He sat down across the table from his old friend. "Well." He looked at Tim, who was eating a piece of toast.

Tim looked up, pushing his sunglasses back on the top of his head.

"It was a new low for you, Tyler. You might have lost some weight in Basic, but I think you added more muscle. I had a hell of a time carrying you to the cabana."

"So what did I do? I can't remember, Tim." Lupe arrived with the coffee and juice then left.

"We ended up at the Marina Club. Do you remember that?"

Tyler thought for a minute. "Oh yeah, you met some girls there, right?

"Right. I went off to talk with them and you stayed at the bar. The more you drank the less social you became. You were drinking straight shots of tequila with beer chasers. By the time I got back to you, you were well on your way to oblivion. Then you started talking about your mother and I ruled out the nice ladies I had met, who by the way were willing to chance it with a jarhead like you?"

"I am not a jarhead. That's the Marines, I am a soldier." Tyler moaned remembering now that the girls were cute.

"So what happened next?" Tyler said, not really wanting the answer.

"Oh, you were crying in your beer about your mom being some radical hippie artist. Stuff like that. The problem was you kept drinking the tequila until the bartender cut you off. You wanted to go someplace else, but you eventually passed out in the Vette after yelling at various people whose only sin was walking down the street."

Tyler dropped his head. "Great. I guess I should have told you yesterday how I got kicked off the team. I blacked out that night too.

I did remember going out drinking after we won our fourth game of the season. I was with a group of guys who weren't on the team. Coach McKay had forbidden us to drink during the season, but everybody did. At least I thought that. Anyway I was in this bar totally drunk when I ran into Coach DeWitt. He was the quarterback coach. He told me to leave and that he was going to speak to Coach McKay about my behavior. I swear Tim I don't remember any of this, but evidently I decked him and broke his jaw. I was really lucky I didn't go to jail. DeWitt refused to press charges. When I went into McKay's office the next day a bunch of really mad coaches were waiting for me. A couple minutes later I was off the team."

"Jesus Christ, Tyler, you were on a USC championship team. What were you thinking?" Tim just shook his head.

"The problem, Tim, was that I wasn't thinking. I don't know what happened to me after high school. You were kind of my moral compass in many ways. You hated trouble and for some reason I was always finding it. You seemed to keep me out of it when I was with you." Tyler looked off toward the ocean, tears in his eyes.

Tim sat and looked at his friend. He wasn't sure what to say.

"Well, I guess the easiest answer is for you to slow down on the drinking or maybe think about quitting. I read somewhere that if it gets you into trouble, you shouldn't drink," Tim said, not looking directly at Tyler.

Tyler just nodded. At the moment he was more than beaten down. Here his best friend was going to be a junior at Yale, playing safety on the football team and third base on their baseball team, making good grades and building a future. He was a private in the Army making $79 a month with a very hazy, bleak future in front of him. He had lost the only girl he'd ever loved, his mom was a hippie and his dad was heartbroken. And he thinks I ought to quit drinking.

CHAPTER 8

"You don't have a driver's license? Who in the hell can live in Southern California without driving?" Tyler asked John Raab, who was trying to find a way to Newport Beach from Burbank.

"How in the hell do you usually get around?" Tyler asked.

"I usually walk or run. It's no big deal. I could probably walk there if I can't get a ride." Raab told Tyler. Tyler knew he wasn't kidding. This guy Raab is a strange human, he thought. It had to be at least 50 miles from Burbank to Newport Beach, and he was going to walk he thought.

"I'll pick you up. Just tell me how to get there. I am not real good at finding things in the Valley," Tyler said with a smile.

Raab's parents lived in the typical California tract home built in the 1950s. Tyler thought they all looked the same except for the color on the outside. He had learned a lot about homes from his architect dad. Most of the homes built after World War II were thrown together to capture an influx of migration to the West Coast. Not much thought went into design.

Raab's mother met Tyler at the front door. She was a pleasant looking woman, much older than his mom, he thought. He had learned in Basic that Raab had an older brother who was in prison for burglary. Raab would just shake his head and smile when talking about his brother, Sean. He would pull Tyler in by the shoulder so they were almost face to face.

"He's not too bright, Tyler. Not too bright!"

"Oh Tyler, please come in. John has talked so much about you. I am glad he has found such a nice friend in the Army," Raab's mother said, grabbing his hand and leading him into the living room. Mrs. Raab walked quickly through the kitchen to the backdoor, with Tyler following her. Raab was in a lounge chair reading a book on Russian history, a scene that Tyler found amusing.

"Boning up in case they win the Cold War?" Tyler said as he sat down in a chair opposite his friend.

Raab laid down his book and sat up on the lounge.

"Hey Tyler, you made it. Didn't get lost in the Valley I see," Raab said, ignoring Tyler's question.

"Tyler, I made lunch for you boys before you head back to the beach." Mrs. Raab said before Tyler could reply.

"Oh thanks, Mrs. Raab." Tyler watched her walk back into the kitchen.

"So we're headed to the beach and your surfing empire," Raab said, smiling at Tyler as he stood up and stretched his arms over his head.

"You know I haven't spent much time down there. The old man hates the dampness on the coast, so most of the few vacations we took were to the mountains." Raab pointed east. He paused for a moment and seemed to collect his thoughts.

" When I went into the Army they made me take a psych test. I guess I intentionally answered some of their questions a little unconventionally," Raab said, flashing one of his crooked smiles.

"Anyway, the only thing fun the old man and I ever did in the mountains was hunt once in awhile. The shrink who interviewed me after the test asked me what I liked to do. I told him I like to hunt … alone. I think he almost pissed his pants. He thought I should consider

Special Forces!!" Raab laughed loudly at his own joke. He walked over and patted Tyler on the shoulder.

"Let's get some lunch and get out of here before the old man gets home and you have to listen to his bullshit."

Tyler got the feeling Raab wasn't particularly close to this father.

The ride back to Newport Beach was fun. Raab loved the 'Woody.' He had never been in one before. Tyler was learning that Raab led an almost monastic life. This was a far cry from the materialism that Tyler had grown up with in Orange County.

For not driving or drinking and self imposed isolation, Raab had an endless supply of funny stories that Tyler was beginning to relish. Most were observations of the human condition, but Raab put a spin on the obvious that had Tyler laughing until his sides hurt. His delivery was in the same dry monotone until the end, when he would look seriously at Tyler, like he was sharing his darkest secret, and drop the bombshell ending. Tyler realized this was the therapy he needed in light of everything that had happened to him. Tim was his best friend, but he was much too serious. Raab was like no one he had ever met. Tyler started to make a mental list of his oddities; he didn't drive, didn't drink or smoke, didn't watch T.V. and by far his weirdest trait, he didn't seem all that interested in women. Tim for sure wouldn't understand that one. The other thing Tyler learned during their drive was that Raab was deeply religious and had considered the seminary prior to being drafted. He had never even mentioned faith before today. With all their opposite traits, Tyler thought Raab could maybe help him get his head straight.

"So this is how the other half lives?" Raab said, sounding impressed with Tyler's home.

"You should have seen our place before my mom left and dad had to sell it to get even with her. It was right on the beach," Tyler replied with a moan.

"Well, I can still see sand from here." Raab replied.

It was true. They were only a couple blocks from the ocean. It was a nice home Tyler thought. He just loved the home he had grown up in better.

"Wait till you see Tim's. It's another world all together," Tyler replied, showing Raab his room for the next couple of days. He had told Raab all about his best friend and a lot of the adventures they had shared since grade school.

"It's in Corona del Mar and sits on a cliff overlooking the ocean. They have a full-time maid and gardener to help maintain it. I guess you could technically call it a mansion. You'll see it tonight when we hook up with Tim."

Raab just nodded. Tyler doubted he was impressed. It just wasn't his style.

After storing Raab's stuff, they walked down to the ocean. Tyler hoped he could get in a little surfing before dinner. The waves were only about 3 feet and not worth it, so they walked over to the Balboa Fun Zone and looked at the kids enjoying the rides. After each bought frozen chocolate bananas, Tyler suggested taking the ferry over to Balboa Island. Raab had never been there and was fascinated with the little island community and its tourist shops.

"So do people live here year round?" he asked Tyler as they circled the island's sea wall.

"When I was little, I think these were mostly summer homes," he said, motioning towards the small cottages they were walking by.

"Now they're tearing down a lot of these small ones and replacing them with two-story homes as a primary residence," Tyler lamented. "A couple of years from now and you won't be able to even find a parking place. I wish I had some money, I'd buy now." Back on the ferry, they watched the harbor seals cavort as they swam around the side of the ferry.

Tyler pointed towards the mouth of the harbor. "That's the 'Wedge' on the other side."

Raab could see the rock wall extending out into the ocean. The swells looked big on the other side of it. Even he had heard it was famous for its big waves.

"Many a bodysurfer, including myself, has met his match there," Tyler said, closing his eyes in reflection.

"Do they surf there?" Raab asked.

"Only if you're crazy," Tyler said. "The break is too close to shore. You would kill yourself."

Raab only nodded. He was enjoying his little beach adventure. It beat hanging out at home and listening to his father complain about the state of the Union, like he was some kind of expert on politics, economy and of course the war.

He often wondered if he were adopted. He just didn't fit into his family. His long-suffering mother was always reacting to his dad's latest tirade. She just cleaned up his messes. His brother was always in trouble. He currently was in the Chino Men's Prison for burglarizing a warehouse. The police, responding to a silent alarm, caught Sean and one of his buddies stacking up televisions at the cargo door. He was in his second year of a five year sentence. Raab had only visited Sean once. If it wasn't for the church and his friendship with Father Chuck at St. Matthews, he wondered where he might be. It was Father Chuck who helped him get into Loyola after high school. His dad had just wanted him to go to work.

"Get a job, you lazy bum. You don't need no college to make a buck," was his father's advice.

Father Chuck had helped him get a partial scholarship and a job in the school's cafeteria. He majored in business, but took a lot of religious studies and philosophy courses. He graduated in three and a half years and only did two things the entire time: He studied and ran marathons. Running was his outlet, his private place where he could think clearly.

When he graduated, his counselor -- a young Jesuit -- asked him if he would consider the priesthood. He just wasn't ready, he finally concluded. Instead he took his physical at the L.A. induction center and a couple months later he was a soldier.

He looked over at Tyler and smiled. All his life he had avoided guys like him. The good looking jock who just knew he had life figured out early on; the guy who never waited at the back of the line and always got the good looking girl. That had been his view of people like Tyler. Now he was learning that maybe he had been wrong. Tyler definitely hadn't figured it out; in fact he was pretty screwed up. They could learn from each other, he had concluded. Tyler's friend, Tim, seemed more the stereotype, he thought, at least from Tyler's description.

When they landed at the Balboa dock they walked back to Tyler's home. "Want to meet Tim?" Tyler asked as they approached his 'Woody.'

"Sure, sounds like a plan."

They drove south, down Coast Highway. As they passed the last of the businesses that lined the street , Tyler turned right, toward the ocean. It was a narrow residential street that ended at a large wrought iron gate. Tyler punched in a code and, when the gate opened, Raab found himself looking at one of the largest homes he had ever seen. It was a new design of the old Spanish haciendas he had seen in magazines. Tyler drove on to a tiled circular driveway and parked. The grounds were spectacular. " It looks like a cover for a magazine," he said, drawing a smile from Tyler.

"Actually it's been in Sunset several years ago and a couple other magazines, I think," he said as they got out of the car. Moments later, Tim Rowe walked out the front door.

"Hey, I'm glad you came early," he said. "I was getting bored."

Rowe walked up to Raab and extended his hand.

"You must be Raab. I'm Tim." The two men shook hands.

"Tyler told me you liked being called by your last name. Is that right?" Tim noticed that Raab had very intense eyes that were locked on his. He had not let go of his hand and had stepped very close to him. "Raab is just fine," Raab said, pumping Tim's hand, his eyes softening, but still sizing him up, Tim thought.

"Tyler tells me you're a Yalie and they actually do have a football team that you play on," Raab said, releasing his hand at last and smiling.

"Well not much of a team, but we try," Tim said, assessing the tall, slightly bent Raab, who seemed to be all sinewy muscle.

"Say, do they even have a football team at Loyola?" Tim asked innocently.

"I think we're mostly into basketball, Tim," Raab replied. "How would I know? I washed dishes in the cafeteria on weekends."

"Can a guy get a beer around here?" Tyler interjected, heading toward the front door without waiting for an answer.

After getting beers and a Coke for Raab, Tim led them out to the pool, which sat near the edge of a cliff looking out onto the Pacific Ocean. Raab decided he had never seen a more perfect view of it.

"Well, Tim, how do you manage in New Haven with digs like this to call home? I would never leave the back yard."

Raab looked around surveying the massive backyard and cabana. "I'll take that and call it good," he said.

"I think Tyler claimed that the last time he was here, well at least the bathroom," Tim said, smiling at his own joke. Tyler flushed.

Tim changed the subject right away as he sipped on the cold beer.

"So what would you soldiers like to do tonight here in the great OC?" he asked.

"Well this time I would really like to actually meet some ladies that I would remember in the morning." Tyler said, withholding the impulse to chug his beer.

"Tyler had a little problem last time we met some young ladies," Tim told Raab, who seemed preoccupied. Tim soon saw why: His sister, Chris, was walking out in a red bikini. She walked over and gave Tyler a hug, then turned her attention towards Raab.

"And you are?" she asked, smiling broadly at Raab whose face flushed like he was sunburned.

"Sorry sis, this is John Raab. He's a friend of Tyler's from the Army," Tim said pulling up another chair for his sister.

"John, this is my sister, Chris."

Raab stood and shook hands with one of the most beautiful women he had seen in a long time. He might have held her hand a little too long, he thought.

"So, Tyler, how do you plan on destroying Newport Beach on your leave?" Chris asked Tyler, who was nursing his beer. She had already heard about his first drunken night from her brother. "I thought we could bring you along tonight and I would mind my manners," Tyler said sheepishly.

"Oh great! That's what I need to do, go out with you animals and drink myself into oblivion."

"I don't drink." Raab said quietly.

Chris looked over at Tyler's new friend. "Jesus, he has intense eyes," she thought.

She had to admit he was kind of cute, in a quirky way. He just looked so military.

She was in her first year at Stanford's law school. She had completed her undergraduate degree and was pleased to get into the law school. She had been demonstrating against the war since her junior year and felt funny being around soldiers, even ones she knew.

"OK, I'll go with you, but no uniforms," she said, knowing they never would.

Raab watched as she got up and dived into the crystal water of the pool. She barely made a ripple. She surfaced and looked back at him.

"Listen, I already know everything worth knowing about my brother and Tyler. Why don't you come in here and tell me a little about you," she said, swimming to the shallow end and sitting on one of the steps.

They spent the next couple hours talking about everything and nothing. Raab told her about his studies at Loyola, Basic Training and what he knew of the pending assignment to Fort Riley. He found her not only beautiful, but very smart. He couldn't believe she didn't have a boyfriend.

"I haven't found anyone who can keep up with me," she explained to Raab, who already wanted to apply for the job.

CHAPTER 9

Tyler was glad to see that Raab actually did have an interest in the opposite sex. He got a kick out of watching him try to impress Chris at the night club. Raab could tell a good story, no matter what the subject was. He was a little jealous that Chris seemed attracted to him. He had always had a secret crush on her since high school. She had always treated him like another younger brother.

Tonight, he told himself, I am only sipping beer. No more drunken nightmares. He was lost in his own thoughts when someone tapped him on the shoulder. He turned to see Tami Hillman smiling at him.

"Well hello, soldier boy," Tami said, leaning into the booth. She kissed him lightly on the cheek.

"Tami, please sit down." Tyler pushed her into the booth that held Tim, Raab and Chris. Tami slid in and eyed Tim Rowe, whom she'd had a crush on in high school that had never amounted to anything more than a surfing date now and then.

Tyler introduced her to John Raab and ordered a beer for her after everyone else said hi.

"So what are you doing here?" Tyler asked after she had settled into the booth.

"I heard there were all these good looking guys hanging out here, so here I am."

She smiled coyly at Tim. "Actually I am home for spring break, Tyler; you know my junior year is coming up. The Bruins are going to kick ass on your Trojans this next year now that you're gone."

Tyler just buried his head in his hands in mock remorse. Well maybe not mock, he thought.

Tami went on, without prompting, to the subject Tyler was really interested in -- Patty Olsen Bedford.

"So did you hear about Sam Bedford? He got drafted a couple weeks ago and goes in this month."

Tyler was stunned. "What's Patty going to do?"

"She said she's getting a job and moving back home."

Tyler frowned. "I thought that's why she got married, to get away from them," he said, as Tami nodded in agreement.

"I guess you sometimes do things you later regret, Tyler."

Tyler wondered if there were a couple messages in her answer.

Raab and Chris got up to dance and Tami turned her attention to Tim. "So how's the big Yalie? Not much surf in New Haven, huh?"

"Well why don't we dance and I'll tell you all about it," Tim said, sliding out of the booth and taking Tami's hand.

Tyler sat alone, pondering the news about Patty. Should he call her? Shit, what would he say? "I am still in love with you; leave your husband." Yeah, that would work. He was lost in his thoughts when everyone returned to the table. Tami was hanging onto Tim and Raab was still making goo-goo eyes at Chris. He felt like the odd man out. Maybe he needed another beer.

The rest of his leave went fast. Tyler decided not to interfere with Patty's life and he didn't call her. Raab stayed at his house for most of the time and went out a couple more times with Chris. Tyler spent a lot of time in the water with Tim. Raab tried surfing a couple of times, with hilarious results. He eventually did stand on the board for about 15 seconds, and considered it an absolute success.

After Raab left, he had a long talk with his dad. He was very concerned about Tyler being a medic and going to Vietnam. His father, like his mother, was opposed to the war.

"You know, Tyler, I was too young for World War II and married by the time Korea came around," he said. "I don't understand the military or this war. I just want you to finish your service and get back to school. I'm afraid for you."

His dad hugged him, tears in his eyes. For living in conservative Orange County, he had a lot of liberal relatives and friends.

CHAPTER 10

Tyler stared out the window of the United 727 taking him to Kansas City. Raab sat next to him, deep in sleep. It was clear and he could survey the flat, bleak terrain from 30,000 feet. It was depressing, he thought, not like the beauty of the mountains and ocean where he grew up. He tried reading a book, but quickly became bored and put it down. He had looked up Fort Riley at the library when he was on leave. It was in Northeast Kansas, between Junction City and Manhattan on the Kansas River. There evidently wasn't much else around it but farms. Manhattan at least had a college, Kansas State. It had to have its share of women, he surmised. They had to take another plane from Kansas City to Manhattan after they landed. It was an old prop job; he wasn't looking forward to that flight.

It was early evening when they checked in at the base headquarters.

"You will love your accommodations; they haven't been used since the Korean War," a wise ass corporal advised them as he checked their orders.

"You need to report to the hospital. Someone there will get you to your barracks, I guess. "

They got directions to the hospital and got on a military bus headed in that direction. Irwin Army Hospital looked very much like every other hospital in California. Tyler had envisioned some type of Quonset hut out in a field. Instead here was a multistory modem building on a beautiful landscaped campus. He noted a new dormitory adjacent to it. He wondered what the wise ass corporal was talking about. These looked great from the outside at least.

"Oh, you guys aren't staying there," the sergeant on duty at the hospital reception center told them. "Those are for the enlisted staff here at the hospital. I'll show you your quarters."

They walked for about a half mile, carrying their duffel bags past what appeared to be deserted buildings out of an old World War II movie. The sidewalk ended and they entered an enclosed hallway of what appeared to be a deserted barracks. Sporadic lights along the corridor lit their way until they reached the end of the long building. Tyler could see lights in two of the barracks. The sergeant led them to the last one and entered it. Inside, several soldiers were lying on single beds on both sides of the barracks. . The sergeant motioned toward a row of empty mattresses with bedding piled on them.

"Pick an empty one," he said. "You can get breakfast at the hospital at 0600 then report back here for formation out front at 0700. The rest of your class better be here by then."

The sergeant turned on his heels and walked out, leaving them to stare at a very old barracks. They moved towards the middle of the room and selected two empty bunks beside each other. Tyler tossed his duffle bag on the foot locker at the base of his bed. There was also a standing locker adjacent to the head of the bed. Plenty of room he thought.

"The Army sure didn't spare any expense on this place," Raab said, sitting on the springs of the narrow bed without bothering to lay down the mattress.

Tyler had noticed one of the other trainees had been staring at him since entering the barracks. He had a smirk on his face, seemingly amused at Tyler's presence. He got up from his bunk and walked over.

"Tyler Taylor, big football star, surfer and overall stud," the blond, slightly built soldier said. "I can't believe they got you."

Tyler looked up at young man now standing at the foot of his bunk. "You don't remember me, do you?"

Tyler had a vague impression of knowing this guy, but he didn't know from where. He shrugged his shoulders. "You tell me," he said, keeping his eyes on the young looking soldier, who didn't look exactly friendly.

"Well, Taylor, do you remember a little fight you were in your junior year at Newport Beach High? It was out on the baseball field. You and some of your friends from the football team were going to teach the 'Khaki' boys a lesson."

Tyler remembered right away. It was another one of his low points he would have rather forgotten.

"You're Mike Petrov, right?"

Petrov was one of the real minority kids in a surfing school. He was a 'Khaki Boy'. The would be bad asses of the South Coast. They wore khaki bell bottom pants and "Sir Guy" shirts, always buttoned at the top. Their hair was longish and slicked straight back with Brylcreem. If they had cars, they were a lowered cruisers. Their girlfriends had ratted hair, tons of make-up and short skirts. He had no use for them back then, but lacked any good reason for the beating he and some of his buddies had administered that day. Hell, they were bigger and a lot stronger than any of those losers. After a teacher had broken up the fight, the only ones identified and punished were the 'Khaki Boys'. The administration and teachers didn't like the Khaki's either he figured. Petrov had been a senior then. After he graduated Tyler had never seen him again. Good riddance, he thought.

"You know Taylor, not only did you beat me up that day, I got swatted the next day by Dean Wilson for fighting in addition to a two day suspension. I never got to thank you. Now you walk into my life in a place where we all get guns. Cool."

Petrov turned and walked back to his bunk without waiting for any comment from Tyler.

"Gee, Tyler, making friends already," Raab said, patting Tyler on the shoulder and smiling broadly.

Tyler wondered if would ever get away from his past.

CHAPTER 11

There were about 40 men assembled in the classroom across from their barracks; almost all of them from Fort Ord. Tyler and Raab took seats near the front of the room.

"Men, my name is Sergeant Moore and I will be one of the instructors here for your training to become a medical corpsman." Tyler looked at the very neat and fit 40 something year old sergeant standing in front of them. He would have been a good looking guy except for a nasty scar that ran down his jaw. He was about 5'8 and probably no more than 160 pounds. He blinked his eyes repeatedly as he spoke. "This course will be different than the one you would have received at Fort Sam Houston. It is longer and will have additional specialized training after you complete your classroom studies. All of you are here because you scored higher than most on the intelligence tests you took in Basic Training. I have reviewed your personnel files and I am confident that you can become a qualified medics. Most of you have either completed college or have at least attended a year or more. Having said all of that, you will be tested at the end of each week of training. If you flunk two of these tests, you will be transferred to the Infantry immediately."

Tyler had noted that Moore was wearing the insignia of the 5th

Special Forces Group on his right arm, signifying that he had served with them in combat. He looked more brainy than brawny, Tyler thought. Nonetheless, he had the eyes of a defensive end about to cream a quarterback; no fear, all attitude.

Sergeant Moore then introduced the rest of the cadre, including several officer nurses. Tyler tried to catch the eye of a cute blond lieutenant -- to no avail.

After most of the corpsman/nurse instructors left, they received an overview of their studies. Introduction to anatomy and physiology kept them busy taking notes until lunch. The food at the hospital was by far the best Tyler had tasted in the Army. You actually had a choice of different foods and no one was yelling at you to hurry up and eat. He had just filled his tray when he saw Petrov sitting alone at one of the tables. He motioned to Raab and they sat across from the unsmiling Petrov.

"You know Mike, we Newport Beach High guys need to stick together through all this don't you think?" Tyler said as he took a bite of roast beef.

"You know Taylor; guys like you are the reason guys like me will never go to their high school reunions," Petrov replied. "You probably enjoyed high school. I hated it and all you jocks. I am willing to forget all of that now because you are in the same miserable place that I am." Tyler said nothing and Raab had a concerned look on his face.

"I didn't like high school either, Mike." Raab said in a low voice.

They ate in an awkward silence for several minutes. Tyler stared down at his plate and began to lose his appetite.

"I took a lot for granted in high school, Mike. College, too. That's why I am here now and not playing football. I am sorry for what happen back then. I just hope we can be friends."

Tyler extended his hand across the table; Petrov just stared at it. "You know Taylor, maybe you should try making friends with the other preppy college boys that seem to share our classroom. You wouldn't want to be seen with a loser like me would you?" Petrov rose from the table and left the cafeteria. Tyler still had his hand extended.

Raab gave a nod of his head. "You know Tyler, I believe that boy has some pent up resentment towards you. Give him some time to get to know the "new" Tyler Taylor."

Tyler pushed aside his food. He had definitely lost his appetite. Raab decided to change the subject.

"So what did you think about Sergeant Moore? Did you see the Special Forces patch on his shoulder?" Raab asked Tyler while starting to eat his second dessert.

"I think he's going to kick our asses if we don't do well with our studies. He seemed genuinely interested that we succeed. So far I am impressed with him and the program. Of course it's the first day and if anything can be screwed up, the Army will find a way to do it."

Raab was nodding his head in agreement between bites. "This looks like it's going to be substantially different from basic and all that bullshit. I for one am going to being studying a lot more than I did in college. I sure in the shit don't want to go into the Infantry."

"Hell, Raab, that's where we'll probably end up anyway; we'll just be medics." Tyler looked down and noticed Raab was now working on his third dessert.

"Jesus, Raab, do you run on sugar only?" Tyler had noticed when they were on leave that Raab loved sweets.

Raab looked over at Tyler's dessert still sitting on his tray. "Are you going to eat that?"

Tyler shook his head in amazement and handed the pudding to his friend.

During the next week they settled into the routine of the medical training. On Friday they took their first written test. Tyler felt pretty confident he had done fine. That evening the scores were posted in both barracks for all to see. Raab had 100 percent while Tyler and Petrov were in the high 90s. Sergeant Moore seemed pleased with most of his trainees' scores. He announced there would be an inspection of the barracks in the morning and passes for everyone if they looked sharp for the captain.

The preparation was intense since everyone was sick of the barracks and the classroom. They were anxious to see Junction City or Manhattan and drink a couple beers.

The captain entered at 0800 while each man stood by his bunk at attention. You could tell he was surprised how they had transformed the old barracks into a neat, clean military abode. The floors had been waxed to a high sheen, the beds were so tightly made that a dropped dime would bounce and the latrine was shining.

After looking around and touching everything with his white gloved hand, a little smile came to his face. He turned to Sergeant Moore and said, "Sergeant, I haven't seen a barracks stand this tall since I was in OCS. I would be pleased to provide passes for the weekend to your men. You've done a fine job with them."

After the captain had left, Sergeant Moore had the men gather around him.

"OK, here's the warning for you guys," he said. "Junction City has booze, whores and a lot of cops and MPs. If you get in trouble, you're on your own. My advice is to take it slow until you learn the ropes. For those of you thinking that you'll go to Manhattan for those college girls, you may have another thing coming. They're not too keen on soldiers with all the anti-war sentiment on campus. I know however, that many of you think you'll be the exception. I just say good luck. We start back in the classroom at 0800 on Monday. You best not be late."

Tyler and Raab and stood at the bus station contemplating where to go. Tyler spoke first.

"I'd like to give Manhattan a look first if that's OK with you ."

"Well Sergeant Moore didn't paint a rosy picture of either, so I don't care." Raab answered.

The bus station was a ways from the college district. After receiving directions from a bored clerk at the station, they headed in what they hoped was the right direction. It was late summer and the leaves on the trees were just beginning to turn. It would be the first time any of them had ever experienced a seasonal change. California stayed the same- year round.

Tyler caught sight of the Kansas State football stadium while they were cutting across a city park. A little later they found what they were looking for: a bar that sold sandwiches and pizza. It was a little after noon, but the bar was already crowded. There was an empty table near the back of the bar and they settled in there. After ordering a pitcher of beer, a coke for Raab and a pizza, Tyler took in the surroundings. There appeared to be lots of college kids and very few soldiers gathered at the bar and tables. Most of the males had longish hair and hippy type clothing. Tyler realized that he and his friends stood out like sore thumbs with their short hair and conservative clothes. He was starting to understand a little about prejudice, he thought. He was lost in his own thoughts when the waiter arrived with their drinks. He was pouring himself a beer when he saw Petrov enter the bar. Raab saw him too. "Do you want to try again with him?" Raab asked while looking at the bar's pizza menu.

"Yeah, but maybe it should come from you. I don't think he still likes me very much."

Raab got up from the table and walked over to Petrov who had sat down at the bar. Tyler watched as the two soldiers talked and Raab motion towards him. After talking together for several more minutes, the two walked over to the table. Petrov had a serious look on his face.

After both took seats at the table, Raab spoke. "I told him I didn't like you much either Tyler, but we we're all in this together and maybe after a few beers he could take you out back and kick your ass, with my help of course." Raab was smiling, but Petrov had not changed his expression. Tyler pushed the beer he had poured in front of Petrov. "Can I buy you a beer Mike before you guys kick my ass?"

Petrov looked down at the beer, picked it up and took a long drink. "It doesn't make us instant buddies Taylor, but I'll drink your beer."

Tyler only nodded. The waiter brought another glass and he poured himself a beer. He also took a long swig.

"Jesus, this stuff tastes like water. What the hell did we order?"

Tyler said, holding the beer mug out and looking at it like it had the answer.

Petrov gave him a knowing smile.

"Its 3.2 beer, that's all they sell here. It's much lower in alcohol, Bud's 5.0 in California," he explained to a frowning Tyler.

"Well, Mr. Science, where do you find the hard stuff in this state?" Tyler asked, still contemplating his beer.

"I don't know, let's ask." Petrov motioned to the waiter, who eventually came over. "So where can you get a hard drink?"

The waiter explained that you had to join a private club and bring in your own bottle. The bartender would then mark it with your name and keep in on the back bar. They made their money by selling the club membership and mixes for drinks.

"Great, we have at least 15 more weeks here and we're stuck with this piss beer," Tyler said.

"Hey the Coke tastes just the same," Raab said, giving Tyler one of his crooked smiles and a slap on the back.

The pizza arrived and it was good. They were on their second pitcher of beer when Tyler thought this 3.2 beer might slow down his drinking. He couldn't hold that much of it. After a couple of hours they decided to explore the area around campus. Tyler almost fell over as they exited the bar. There was a station wagon driving slowly past them; it had a surf board tied down to the roof. The two occupants had long blond hair and were wearing sunglasses.

"Holy shit, we're two thousand miles from the ocean. What's the deal?" Tyler wondered, shaking his head.

"We're not in Kansas anymore, Dorothy," Raab said, laughing at his own joke.

They walked around for more than an hour. Kansas State was playing at Colorado for their season opener. Tyler picked up a copy of their schedule, figuring ; maybe he would attend a game. It dawned on him that this was the first year he hadn't played football since junior high school. Another thing that had changed: coeds were no longer giving him the eye like at USC. He was no longer a big man on campus, just another lonely soldier out of his element.

"Let's find another bar," he said as the group walked back towards the bus station.

CHAPTER 12

The weeks of medical training passed quickly. The instructors covered every conceivable wound they might encounter and the treatment for it. After an entire day on tropical disease, Tyler's head was spinning. He had a new outlook on what it must take to be a physician.

They were nearing the end of the classroom portion of the training and in a couple weeks would be assigned to various areas in the hospital for more advanced work. Just the week before, he had been laughing out loud as he watched one of the young medics trying to give his first shot to Raab.

Private Abrams was a Jewish kid who couldn't stand the sight of blood. He was shaking so hard he could barely find Raab's arm. When he finally did, he pushed in the needle so slowly that the agonized Raab was begging him to finish. After Abrams passed out when the class learned how to draw blood, Sergeant Moore had him transferred to the base Veterinary Clinic. Tyler guessed that Moore figured animals wouldn't be as traumatized by Abrams. They couldn't think about what was coming, unlike his buddy Raab.

In the last week the class practiced loading and unloading

helicopters. If they became combat medics, this would come in handy, Tyler thought. He enjoyed the rides in the Huey helicopters in simulated combat conditions. After taking their final written test, Sergeant Moore addressed them.

"After your next eight weeks of advanced medical training you will be reassigned to your next duty station," he said. "Some of you will remain stateside working in Army hospitals, however the majority of you will probably be sent to Vietnam. For those of you who are a little more adventurous and want to put off Nam a little longer, I can offer you the opportunity to participate in airborne training. The airborne units are in need of qualified medics. You would be assigned to either Fort Benning or Fort Bragg for the three weeks of training. If you do go to Vietnam, it will at least be with an elite outfit. I don't need an answer right away; you have two days to decide."

Later that night Tyler, Raab and Petrov were drinking beer at the Bottoms Up, one of the Go-Go clubs in Junction City. They had long given up any expectations of fitting in with the college crowd in Manhattan. The only exception was Petrov, who met a co-ed who actually went out with him. So far he was the only one in their group to get laid. Tonight they were getting bored watching a bikini clad woman dancing in a cage suspended above the bar.

"So why don't we all go airborne together?" Tyler asked nonchalantly as he sipped his beer.

"Taylor, are you crazy? Why in the world would you want to jump out of a perfectly good airplane?" Petrov said, slamming down his beer mug, his eyes flashing. He still wasn't sure about Tyler, but was gradually warming up to him.

Raab, on the other hand, was smiling . "You know, Mike, it might be fun," he said. "At least we'd be out of this God forsaken state. I heard those Southern girls like GIs. Tyler might even get laid. After eight more weeks here, I know I'll be ready for a change. Sergeant Moore's right I think. If you have to go, it might as well be with an elite outfit. I'll go with you, Tyler."

Petrov looked at both of them as if they had gone insane.

"If we go airborne, you know we will end up in Nam," he pleaded.

"Shit, Mike, we were going to Vietnam the minute we hit this man's Army," Tyler said. "Don't you get it? Besides that no one gets along with you but me and Raab. Who the hell will you bitch to about everything?"

Raab stood up holding his Coke and started singing, "I want to be an airborne ranger, live a life of love and danger."

Soldiers from all around the bar started to boo Raab's performance. Beer cans were thrown and Raab ducked down avoiding several well placed throws.

"Well I still think we should give it a try, Mike," Raab said as he wiped beer off his shirt.

Petrov slowly nodded his head. "In this case, I probably won't live to regret it anyway."

The next morning the three friends stood in front of Sergeant Moore in his office.

"To be honest men, I didn't think I would get any takers," Moore said. "You three don't surprise me though, well I should say, with the exception of Petrov. I didn't see you volunteering for anything." He made direct eye contact with Petrov.

"So far you three are the only ones to see me about this. I'll process the orders once you sign the request forms. You'll also need to take a physical readiness test, so you may want to start running again. You may have noted we haven't had much physical training since you have been here."

It was true, Tyler thought, he hadn't done much more than the pick-up tag football games on the weekends. Raab of course had been running every evening after class. Tyler figured that he and Petrov better start joining him.

They each signed the appropriate forms. Moore said he would keep them together for the remaining eight weeks of advanced training. They were to start in the emergency room. Sergeant Moore followed them as they filed out of the office. "By the way men, you're all being promoted to private first class," he said. "Congratulations!"

The 9th Infantry Division was getting ready to deploy to Vietnam from Fort Riley. The nights working in the emergency room were eye opening for the three newly minted medics. The closer the division came to shipping out, the more self inflicted injuries they saw. In one three day stretch the department treated four gunshot wounds, two stabbings and a half dozen drug overdoses. One sorry soldier actually managed to kill himself by running into a stone wall near the PX. The Army ruled it an accident, but most knew it wasn't. Tyler started to recognize the fear he saw in all of their eyes. Death seemed easier than taking their chances in the jungle. The MPs who brought in most of them treated them with contempt. The commanding officers who were summoned to the ER to confront their troops treated them as non-humans. Tyler felt sorry for some of them; they just didn't belong in the Army for a variety of physical and mental reasons. But no one gave them any sympathy and most were returned to their units for deployment. Tyler was starting to think his decision to go airborne was a good idea. He wouldn't want to be in the field with these losers they were returning to the 9th. The airborne soldiers would be motivated; at least he hoped so.

One of the skills they picked up in the ER was learning to suture wounds. The ER docs were more than willing to let the medics sew up wounds. After starting endless IV drips, Tyler was pretty sure he had that down too. One of the veteran medics told him, "Wait until you do that under fire lying in the dirt; that's when it counts. "

Tyler only nodded. He had learned to listen and respect the medics who had already survived a tour in Nam.

After four weeks in the ER, Tyler, Raab and Petrov were transferred to a general surgical operating room. For the next two weeks, they watched and listened to the surgeons as they operated on everything from gallstones to cancer.

They also saw one accidental gunshot wound that had occurred during live fire training. The young soldier lying on the operating table had been shot in the upper thigh. The surgeon showed how to debride the wound by removing the dead tissue from it. He would check if the flesh was viable by squeezing it with the forceps and releasing it. If the blood returned to the section of flesh after release; it was retained. The mushy flesh lacking blood was cut out. Tyler was amazed at the extent of damage inflicted by a single M -16 bullet. He doubted he would ever be in a position to do surgery on a gunshot wound, but who knew what the future held for him and his friends. This training certainly wouldn't hurt.

The last two weeks were served in the hospital pharmacy. They learned more than they ever wanted to know about pharmacology and the ever present Physician Desk Reference, or PDR for short. The pharmacist who supervised them gave homework assignments nightly requiring additional readings about drugs and their interaction with the human body. He and his friends each carried a PDR everywhere they went.

Towards the end of their eight weeks at the hospital, they received their orders for jump school. They were going to Fort Benning in Georgia.

Tyler was lying on his bunk starting to read a letter he had been holding for a week without opening it when Petrov walked up.

"Hey, you want to do another fun night in Junction City? Raab's going on one of his extended runs and I hate to drink alone."

"I don't think so, Mike," Tyler said, sitting up on his bunk. "I think I've had it with that sorry town. I need to catch up on my letter writing before we ship out." He held up the letter he had been holding as if to prove his point. He was happy that after all these weeks of training, Petrov had finally warmed up to him.

"OK, but if I get in trouble, remember it's your fault for not going with me," Petrov said, walking out and leaving Tyler alone in the barracks.

Most of the others had received their orders and duty assignments. About ten of their class were going to Vietnam right after a leave.

Tyler lay back down and began reading the letter from his mother. She had been writing him weekly and he had yet to write her back. She always said the same thing, wanting him to write or call her. She sounded more desperate with each letter. Tyler knew she was scared to death he would end up in Nam.

He dropped her letter on the floor and closed his eyes, trying to remember when everything had first gone to shit for him. He realized he always had a mean streak in him. Why, he wondered? He certainly had a great upbringing. It was very different from the other soldiers he had met since entering the service. Lots of poor men with very little education, black guys from the ghetto who would never understand what it was like growing up rich in Orange County. He had thrown so much away.

It was starting to dawn on him that he could change and really make a future for himself. Hell he had cut his drinking in half and had managed to stay out of fights. There was always some soldier in the bars who had drunk too much and thought he was Muhammad Ali. Most of the fights he saw were between Southern whites and inner city blacks. It was too bad, he thought. Someday they may need to rely on each other in combat.

His thoughts jumped all over but finally landed on what he was trying to avoid thinking about -- Patty. She crossed his mind every day in some way. He had gotten a letter from Tami Hillman several weeks ago. She told him in it that Sam Bedford was in Basic Training and Patty had moved back home. He called her at her parents, but hung up after the first ring. His radio was playing "California Dreamin.'" Whoever wrote that song must have been in Kansas. He found himself growing more melancholy and turned it off. Maybe he should have gone with Petrov. He reached down and retrieved his mother's letter from the floor. After reading it again, he took out his notepad and pen and started writing. "Dear Mom," he began.

CHAPTER 13

Tyler stepped off the plane in Columbus, Georgia, and felt like he had entered a sauna. It had to be at least 90. The heat wasn't what bothered him; it was the humidity. He was soaked by the time he entered the terminal with Raab and Petrov. It had been a chilly fall day when they said goodbye to Kansas. Now he was in the land of "y'alls."

They found a bus to Fort Benning. The driver pointed out the Chattahoochee River and other city highlights along the way.

"Yeah, this is going to be fun, Tyler." Petrov sulked in his now wet Class A uniform.

"Think of it this way, Mike," Raab said, looking out the window. "We'll be adjusted to the weather in Nam before they even send us."

They were assigned to the 1st Battalion (Airborne) 50th Infantry Regiment, Basic Airborne Course. After checking in they were issued airborne boots and other equipment and after finding their training company, they found bunks together in the enlisted men's barracks.

"I wonder if the officer's barracks are air conditioned?" Petrov asked.

"I bet they are, Mike," Tyler said. "Probably have beer on tap and a steady supply of women to keep them company. However, think of it this way, we're getting a heads up on them."

"How's that, Taylor?"

"Well, we will be used to this miserable weather by 0500 tomorrow when we start training. I bet we can plan on the airborne shuffle right out of the box."

Tyler was unfortunately correct about the start of their first day. It was a five mile run, followed by an hour of PT.

Sergeant Calloway reminded Tyler of Sergeant Crooker from Basic Training; mean, lean and gung ho.

"Men, during your first week of training we will be weeding out the unmotivated and weak among you," Calloway said. "Our program here is designed to prepare you to make a parachute jump and land safely. This week your platoon will train on the mock door, the 34 foot tower and lateral drift apparatus. If you fail any of the requirements, you will be through with this training immediately. We are not your mommas and will not be pampering you. Do you understand?"

"Yes, sergeant!" The assembled men shot back in unison.

Tyler was very glad that he and Petrov had been running nightly with Raab in Kansas. At least the Army was providing water. He seemed to be sweating out everything he took in and then some.

After a morning of nothing but physical training, the afternoon was spent in the classroom. It was also no surprise to find out the three of them were the only medics in their platoon. Tyler figured they were probably the only ones in the whole company. The majority of men were from the Infantry. The day ended with another run and the constant singing of "I want to be an airborne ranger." Petrov summed it up that night after lowering himself into a seat at the regimental mess hall.

"You know, Tyler, I think my original thought of killing you when I first saw you in Kansas was right. I am going to kill you!!!"

"Mikey, Mikey, that's no way to talk," Raab said. "Just look at all this free food and the abundance of fresh air and exercise you're getting thanks to Tyler." Raab said in reply.

"OK, so maybe wasn't the best idea I ever had," Tyler chimed in.

He was very sore and this was just the first day. "I just thought it might be a good way to get over my fear of heights."

Tyler laughed. Jesus, he thought, now I am picking up Raab's self deprecating warped sense of humor.

The first week ended with a test on the 34-foot tower and PT test and the 4-mile run. They all managed to complete all the requirements with not a lot of strain. The four mile run for time saw several applicants failed, but they all qualified easily. They were also introduced to their next new best friend -- the parachute. Tyler was amazed the cadre didn't make them sleep with them on. And after exiting the mock plane door about 20 times, Tyler was pretty certain they had it down. He had actually enjoyed the 34 foot tower jump, though it was over too quickly. So ended ground week.

Tyler was starting to see a pattern in cities that were near military bases; the urban blight brought on by too many bars, prostitutes, drugs and soldiers facing the possibility of death. Columbus had been a Southern mill town that by the 60s had seen its best years. Now it relied on the soldiers' money. It brought in the criminal element, hustlers and the other parasites hoping to make a buck on a bunch of gullible young men, most of whom were away from home for the first time.

Columbus and Manhattan were Tyler's first real exposure to cities outside the west coast. While at USC, he had traveled to a lot of cities for their games. But there was very little access to the cities outside of hotel rooms and stadiums. The coaches made sure of that.

One night Tyler, Raab and Petrov found themselves in yet another GI bar, with all the vices very apparent. It could have been Junction City all over again with the go-go dancers, pimps and whores. The exception was he and Petrov were drinking Jack Daniels; not 3.2 beer. Raab as usual stuck to Coke, though he was tempted to try it with rum, at Petrov's urging.

"I guess we'll be getting orders next week for our next duty station." Raab said to nobody in particular. Sergeant Moore had told them at Fort Riley that the airborne training was a temporary duty assignment and their ultimate assignment would come near their completion of that training.

"Anybody want to bet it's not Vietnam?" Petro asked.

"You know Mike, we could already be there getting our asses shot off instead of enjoying this quiet moment in beautiful downtown Columbus," Tyler said. The sound system playing "Wild Thing" drowned out most of Petrov's salty reply.

The bar was full of soldiers, some in their khaki, short sleeve uniforms. Tyler noted many had airborne wings over Vietnam service ribbons and combat infantryman badges. Most of the veterans just drank and kept to themselves. He had learned it was best not to bother them. While at Fort Riley he and Raab tried to engage one of the Green Berets they ran into at the bus station in a conversation about Nam. He stared off as if he were in a trance, and then looked hard at both of them.

"You want to talk about Nam? When you get back, look me up, then we'll talk," he said. "Right now you assholes don't even have a reference point."

With that, he turned and walked away from them.

Tonight they would just try to avoid making eye contact with the silent group of combat vets sitting next to them, who all appeared lost in their own thoughts. It wasn't like he was afraid of them, Tyler thought. They just deserved to be left alone.

About midnight they got bored and headed back to the base. A black guy caught up to them on one of the side streets they had turned down, assuming it was a short- cut to the bus station.

"Hey man, you guys looking for some pussy, because you came to right place?"

Tyler had stopped to face the 30-something year old who was now blocking his path. He had an ugly pock-marked face.

"We're not interested, man," Tyler answered for the group.

When he tried to move past him, the man again tried to block his path.

"What are you white boys doing down here then if you're not looking for pussy," he said, looking daggers at Tyler while ignoring Raab and Petrov. "Take a wrong turn?"

His next mistake was pushing Tyler in the chest. Tyler dropped him with a very quick right cross, breaking his nose. Tyler wasn't through. He pulled the man up from the ground only to punch him in the gut, followed by another blow to the face. This time the man went down for good. Raab knelt down to check his vitals. The man was unconscious, but breathing. Raab turned him on his side to keep the blood from pooling on his face.

"I don't think you killed him, Tyler," Raab said. "Close; but no kill. Think we might want to get out of here," he added, noticing his friend was still holding his fists high, ready for more.

"I think in the future we might want to avoid that short-cut. What do you think, Tyler?" Petrov said as they boarded the bus for the base. He was startled at Tyler's quickness with his fists.

"Well ,Tyler, new town and some more new friends," Raab said with a laugh, putting his arm around Tyler as they settled into a seat on the bus.

Tyler was still pumped up as they rode in silence towards Fort Benning. "Jesus, I thought I was getting my temper under control."

"So are you OK? Raab asked as the bus plowed through the darkness. Petrov, who was sitting in the seat in front of them turned back and answered for Tyler:

"Shit, John, how could he get hurt? The pimp was the only one feeling any pain."

Tyler said nothing, just slumping down further in the seat. "Maybe I should have kept with the 3.2 beer," he thought. He had felt no pain after about the third Jack Daniels that night. Anger and drinking, maybe there is a correlation he thought, already knowing the answer.

Raab rose early and had the shower to himself. His two friends and most of the company were still fast asleep when he left to find the base chapel for Mass. The chapel was used for all the denominations at Fort

Benning. The priest's assistant was setting up the altar for the Catholic service when Raab took a seat near the back of the chapel. He was the first one there and Captain Joe O'Rourke, the Catholic priest, walked up and greeted him.

Raab introduced himself, standing at near attention.

"John, come on up front. We may not have a big turnout this early on Sunday. You know some of the boys like to sleep in after their Saturday night shenanigans. Where are you from, John?"

"Burbank, California, Father, I am here for airborne training."

"Well, how is it going, John?" The priest asked.

"I just completed my first week. It's hard, but so far so good." Father Joe patted him on the shoulder.

"I am glad you're here today, John. May the Lord be with you during your training."

Raab repositioned himself in the second row of pews as Father Joe greeted other soldiers as they took their seats. He was lost in his prayers when the Mass started. He had been praying for his two friends; and for the pimp Tyler had dispatched.

"The Lord be with you,"

Father Joe spread his arms in greeting

"And also with you," answered the 20 or so soldiers who were standing throughout the chapel.

Raab knew that neither Tyler nor Mike were particularly religious. Tyler had told him he had been brought up a Methodist. He didn't think Mike ever attended church. It was a subject neither had broached.

Since entering the service, Raab tried to keep up with his devotional prayer at night when he found peace just lying in his bunk. He would think about his strange family, his friends and his calling to the priesthood. During those times he tried not to think about Chris Rowe. Under other circumstances he knew they could be close -- very close. It was those thoughts that made him question whether he should even be thinking about becoming a priest. He was always intrigued with the prospect of a wife and family. Up until now he had never met a woman that piqued that interest like Chris did. And yet, he told himself, he hardly knew her.

After Mass he walked slowly back to the barracks. His two friends were still sleeping when he arrived.

CHAPTER 14

Michael Alexander Petrov really wasn't asleep when Raab entered the barracks. His eyes were closed, but he was deep in his own thoughts. He found himself drifting back into his past. His father, Nicholas, was the only son of Russian immigrants from Moscow.

He was spoiled by his parents and provided for beyond their means. His father, Nicholas, graduated from UCLA in the spring of 1940 and married his mother, a fellow student. They had two daughters prior to World War II.

After the start of the big war, his dad had been drafted and sent to Officers Candidate School. Because he was fluent in Russian, he was assigned to Army Intelligence. He never came close to a bullet while stationed in Europe for most of the war. To hear his stories, though, you would have thought he had single handedly won the war, Mike thought.

Nicholas returned to California and his family after the war and soon found himself in banking, where his love of money and wealth began in earnest.

Mike was born in 1945. Right away he must have been all wrong for his proud father. Unlike his dad, who had dark features, black hair and brown eyes, Mike was fair like his mother. He had light blond hair and blue eyes. His dad had suggested to him on more than one occasion that he was the milkman's son.

For the most part, Mike was just ignored by his father. The family did prosper under his father's unrelenting drive for success and in the late '50s they moved to Newport Beach from Pasadena. Mike, who was shy and reclusive by nature, became more so. Always on the slight side, he was always the little guy in class and sports. By the time he entered high school, he had even given up on baseball, which had been his passion.

He found himself hanging with the other rejects, soon finding he was classified as a 'Khaki' boy. It was the low end of the social ladder at Newport Beach High School. He and his friends were bitter, angry and a little dangerous. They started out with acts of vandalism. When that got too boring, they went onto burglarizing nearby homes. When they split up the proceeds, he would store his share under his parent's home. He had no use for the junk; he just liked the thrill of stealing it. He and his two best friends, Daniels and Garcia, swore never to rat on each other if they were caught.

That pledge lasted about two minutes the day the Newport Police picked up Garcia.

They had received a tip from a friend of Garcia's, who had some police problems of his own. He was only too happy to give up Garcia for lenient treatment. Garcia, given the same deal, told the police all about Petrov and Daniels. It worked that way with criminals, Petrov had learned.

He was removed from his third period class by two plain clothes detectives and taken to the dean's office. His parent's were called and when a mortified Nicholas Petrov arrived, Mike knew that maybe going to Juvenile Hall wouldn't be as bad as going home with him. Throughout the interrogation he had insisted he was innocent and denied knowing anything about any criminal activities or stolen property.

His mother arrived about an hour into the questioning. He was starting to feel pretty smug about not giving up anything, even after being told that Daniels had also confessed. That feeling only lasted about a minute after his mother told the detectives she had found the stolen property under their house. She had evidently searched the entire house after she had been contacted by the police. While walking around the exterior of their house, she noticed the door to the crawl space looked like it had been recently moved away from the house. She was amazed at what she found after crawling under the house.

Two weeks later he found himself standing in front of a Juvenile Court judge. Since it was his first offense, he was given probation, over his father's objection. Nick wanted him in jail. He came close to being kicked out of school, but again was given a second chance. He was, after all, only 14 years old.

The rest of high school, he kept clean. He was still a 'Khaki' boy, but the criminal element was over. Most of the kids at school still thought of him as some sort of gangster, however. His dad never forgave him, Mike would retreat to his bedroom whenever Nick came home.

Mike attended junior college after graduation. His grades were not that bad and he could have got into a four year college, but Nick wouldn't help him financially. He had always been good at math and considered being an engineer of some type. But after two years at Orange Coast College he no idea what he wanted to do with his life. He and his friend, Danny Argeo, decided to volunteer for the draft. They had been told they could serve together. Another Army lie. Argeo was now in the Infantry and assigned to a unit in Germany. They weren't even in Basic Training together.

Now he found himself with the first new friends he had made in years. If someone had told him in high school that he would be friends with Tyler Taylor, he would have thought they were crazy. And Raab; what could you say about him? He was by far one of the most unusual humans he had ever met. The other issue for him had always been that he was small. But he had grown five inches and gained 50 pounds at the end of his senior year. He was an even six feet now and weighed 170 pounds. Finally everyone wasn't looking down at him. He felt himself an equal with Raab and Taylor. He was proving something to himself -- and maybe Nick -- with this airborne training. He would be with the best and now the khakis he wore were provided by the Army.

CHAPTER 15

The second week of airborne school started just like the first: daily physical fitness training along with the long runs in the Georgia heat and humidity. They practiced with more apparatus, including the swing landing trainer used to teach the cadets how to deal with oscillation and landing falls. Tyler noted that the instructors never mentioned what to do if your chute failed to open. Just pray, he guessed.

He had noticed that a lot of would-be paratroopers were short. He had always had a vision of John Wayne's big frame standing in the open door of the airplane, urging his troops to jump. A lot of these guys were really small. During one of their exercises on how to recover from parachute drag after you land, he saw one of the smaller men dragged about 150 feet before getting control of his chute. Nobody laughed at the time, but he and Raab had a chuckle later that night.

The good news for Tyler was never hearing anything about the guy he had beat up on Saturday night. He half expected to see MPs driving up to arrest him at any time.

"No way, he won't say anything," Petrov said. "It's the cost of doing business for those guys."

The week ended with a parachute jump from the 250 foot tower. Tyler thought it was a kick, like surfing the big waves of Hawaii. He allowed himself to think of the days he and Tim Rowe spent surfing almost every island during their summer stays at Tim parent's condo on Oahu. And that first time they finally got the nerve to surf the Pipeline and the rush of adrenaline that followed. He could feel it even now. Maybe jumping out of a plane could duplicate that feeling. He decided it would be a kick no matter what.

By jump week, Tyler and his friends were tired of just training. They were ready to jump out of a plane. After a review of malfunctions and aircraft orientation, they finally were loaded on a C-130 Hercules. They were pumping each other up for what would be the first of five qualifying jumps that week. Their graduation would be held Friday at Eubanks Field. Today their target jump was to be the Fryar Field Drop Zone.

Tyler felt his stomach get queasy as the plane climbed and banked to the east, gaining attitude for the jump. The jumpmaster moved among them, checking chutes and giving words of encouragement. Tyler looked over at Petrov, who seemed lost in his own thoughts. Raab sat next to him, the ever-present smile on his face.

"Tyler, you look a little worried," Raab said. "What's the worst thing that could happen? You die and don't have to go to Nam."

Raab slapped him on the back just as the jumpmaster yelled for everyone to get up and face the door. They clipped on their static lines and waited, but not for long. Tyler was the third jumper out of the door.

It happened very quickly, leaving little time to think before he was floating down towards earth. It was peaceful, he thought, and any stress he felt was gone. It was like riding a wave. The ride down was like the kick-out. About the time he was starting to relax, the ground was coming up fast. He adjusted his chute for the landing and was able to maintain his balance, landing standing up. After collecting his chute, he found Raab and Petrov. Both were fine and smiling.

"Shit, that was a kick," Petrov yelled as Tyler approached.

The Army had managed to keep the whole company intact. A good sign, thought Tyler. They made three more jumps that week, some with full combat equipment, including fake guns. On Friday morning, they would make their final jump, qualifying them for airborne wings. But by Thursday night they had yet to receive any orders for their next assignment. They knocked on Sergeant Calloway's door after dinner.

"Sergeant, what would be our status, not having any orders?" Tyler asked.

"Well men, you came from a training company and I can't send you back there," Calloway said. "I have a feeling the Army wanted to make sure you completed your airborne training before giving you another assignment. After you graduate tomorrow you will be moved to a transient barracks until we get orders for your next assignment."

They all must have looked discouraged.

"The good news is you will have no duty assignments and basically you can lie around all day or go to town if you want," Calloway said. "Hopefully by the end of the week we'll have this sorted out."

As they started to leave his office, Calloway motioned them back.

"You know, I see a lot of soldiers go through this training," he said. "I want you to know that you men did medics proud this last three weeks. I watched you work hard, not complain and keep up with everyone, including the Rangers and Special Forces candidates. I wish you well wherever you end up."

The compliment took all of them by surprise. Usually training sergeants don't give out much praise. They all thanked Sergeant Calloway and shook hands with him.

The next day, after completing their final jump, they were awarded their wings.

"Finally something on the uniform besides the National Defense Ribbon, the lone decoration besides the marksmanship medal," Raab noted as they checked into the transient barracks with several other soldiers who also waiting for orders.

That night they celebrated at what had become their favorite bar in Columbus, The Night Owl.

Raab leaned back in his chair, a big grin on his face,

"So, Mike, what did you think about as you floated down today?"

Petrov looked backed with a serious frown, and then took a sip of his beer.

"I thought about how crazy I was to let you guys talk me into this," he said. "And then again I thought it was kind of fun and totally different from anything else I've done. "

So what were you thinking about?" Petrov asked Raab.

"Hell, I was just praying I would make it to the ground in one piece."

Tyler returned to the table after an extended trip to the restroom and slid into the booth next to Petrov.

"I was just talking to a guy at the bar," Tyler said. "He just got his orders for Vietnam. Going to the 173rd Airborne. According to him they are the only unit to make a combat jump in the war. And get this; it was called Operation Junction City, named after our last drinking hole."

"You know, Taylor, if you paid attention during our classroom training, you would have already known that," Petrov said with a smug smile.

"I was probably daydreaming," Tyler acknowledged.

"Well ,it was last February, Tyler," Petrov said. "You remember last February don't you? It was when we got into this man's Army."

Tyler just nodded. A lot had happen in just eight months, he thought. By October, they would probably be in Vietnam. He hoped they would at least have a short leave before that.

It didn't take that long to find out. On the Wednesday after the completion of airborne training they were summoned to Sergeant Calloway's office.

"I have a couple things for you men," he said. "Your orders have come in. It's Vietnam. Raab and Taylor, 173rd Airborne, Petrov, you're going to the 25th Infantry. Also you have all been promoted to Specialist/4."

"Sergeant, where is the 25th and how come it's not an airborne unit?" Petro asked, disappointed he wasn't staying with Raab and Taylor.

"The 25th Infantry is near Saigon," Calloway said. "I don't know why you were assigned to them. I just pass out the orders Petrov. Men they are both outstanding units." Calloway said as he handed each of them their orders. Tyler glanced down and saw they didn't have to report until Oct. 8. At least they had a little more than a couple weeks leave.

"You can get out of here as soon as you can and start your leave," Calloway said. "I wish you all well, go kick some ass. Wait a minute, in your case, go save some sorry ass."

After a couple of connecting flights and some fifteen hours later, they were back in Los Angeles. They had 18 days before reporting to the Oakland Army Base. Tyler intended on enjoying the time.

"Mind if I hang out at your place for awhile?" Raab asked Tyler as they collected their duffel bags from baggage claim. "It's a lot more fun than Burbank."

"Sure, when do you want to come over? I'll pick you up." Tyler answered.

"I probably need to spend a week at home first. You know, say all my goodbyes just in case. How about picking me up next week sometime?"

Tyler agreed and Raab was off to find his parents. Tyler and Petrov located Tyler's dad and they headed off to Newport Beach. After a quiet car ride and dropping Petrov off at his home, Tyler's dad spoke up.

"Tyler I spoke to your mother yesterday after you called," he said. "She is worried sick about you going over there. I find myself watching the evening news now, hoping somehow it will end. It doesn't and the casualties just keep mounting. Anyway she wants to visit us here before you leave. I told her it would be OK. I hope you agree."

Something told Tyler he should see her and he told his dad that it would be fine.

"Good, because she will be here tomorrow," his dad said.

After unpacking, his duffel bag, Tyler looked around his room. All his old treasures were right where he had left them, but somehow he didn't fit in anymore. His surfboard was in its rack in the garage next to his' Woody'. All so familiar-but not....

He couldn't quite put his finger on the feelings that now pulsed through him. Somehow he felt very lonely and scared. Vietnam seemed so foreboding. He had a knot in his stomach when he finally got into his wetsuit, grabbed the board and headed for the Pacific once again.

"Jesus," he thought, "will this be my last couple weeks of surfing?"

He was sad because he wouldn't be able to see Tim Rowe. He was back at Yale, playing football games. Tyler had followed his season in the newspapers. Yale was playing Holy Cross this weekend and Tim would be back making interceptions, he thought. His old team, USC, was playing Washington State. That's where he really belonged. Or did he?

Then it dawned on him. I am tired of being mad -- mad at myself, my mom and deep down ,mad at Patty for marrying. He was so lost in thought, a wave washed over him, hurling him and his board towards the shore. Tyler recovered and paddled back out.

I have to see Patty before I go, he told himself. Even if it does hurt. He couldn't change all that had happen in his life, but he was determined to rid himself of his self destructive ways.

CHAPTER 16

Raab gazed out the window at a scene much like what he had seen in Kansas. The ranches and farmland all looked the same regardless of the state, he thought. The tranquil setting just didn't mirror his mood or destination. He was headed to the Chino Institution for Men. It was a fancy name for a state prison. It sounded like some college, he thought. It was a level 1 prison with open dormitories without a secure perimeter. His brother wasn't violent...just a drug addict and thief. For that reason, he was allowed contact visits.

His mother had said little since leaving Burbank. She concentrated on her driving, tracing a route she had driven many times before to see her oldest son. Raab didn't want to go, but she kept on him until he agreed. It was a little better than sitting around the house, waiting for the old man to get home from work. He just hated going into the prison

"Hey, John, Jesus it's good to see you," an animated Sean Raab told his younger brother and mother after sitting down on the other side of a long table where other prisoners also were visiting with family members. "I heard you went airborne, man that's what I want to do when I get out of here. you know."

John Raab shook his brother's hand and sat down opposite him at a small table. The room had about 6 other areas where family members could meet with prisoners. Open contact with visitors was restricted to non-violent inmates. At least Sean had never crossed into violent crime, Raab thought.

"You know, Sean, you can't get into the military with a felony conviction," John Raab said, knowing his brother was well aware of that fact.

"Well, maybe it will change when I get out," Sean said. "Anything can happen, John. Hell, maybe the Army will need some specialized help and I could be it you know."

"I doubt they will need burglars, Sean."

As usual , Raab noted, his brother was back at one of his fantasies. When he was arrested the last time, Sean had told him he was stealing for the poor people. The reality was he stole to support his heroin habit. He decided to change the subject.

" I'm going to Vietnam, Sean. I'll be with the 173rd Airborne in the Central Highlands. Maybe you can write me?"

"Oh, he will," his mother answered for her son.

"Yeah, John, I'll write you," Sean said. "I've been keeping up on the war, you know. I read the newspapers and we get TV once in awhile you know."

Why did his brother end every sentence with "you know? " John Raab wondered.

His mom must have sensed his annoyance, as she took over the chit-chat with Sean. It gave John time to take in his surroundings. There were about a dozen prisoners in the cramped room, meeting with friends or loved ones. What a waste, he thought. He could never imagine being in prison. For his brother, it was just a break from the outside world. He doubted it bothered him at all to be here. He, on the other hand, was already feeling a little claustrophobic.

After an hour the guard stepped forward to take Sean back to his cell.

"You be careful over there, John," Sean said over his shoulder. " I'll be praying for you, you know." Sean said as the guard led him away.

"Thanks, Sean," Raab said, wondering if his brother ever prayed for anything but his next fix.

Back at the car, his mother started talking on about how nice the visit was and didn't Sean look good and how he was up for a probation hearing in just six months. Raab felt sorry for his long suffering mother. He said a silent prayer for her and wondered how long he needed to stick around home before joining Tyler at his house.

He knew if he survived Vietnam, he would never return home. His father, the union organizer, seemed to have more in common with Sean than he ever did. They rarely agreed on any issue. His dad mocked him for his strong faith. He ridiculed the Catholic Church, the pope and almost everything to do with his fleeting thoughts about joining the priesthood. His father thought he was weak.

"I bet you think you're Mister Hotshot now that you have that college diploma," His dad had said recently, during one of their rare confrontations. "Well it don't mean shit, boy. What you need is a good union job where you actually have to work, not be some preacher living off the charity of his congregation and never getting his hands dirty."

That was the advice he received after graduating from Loyola. It was his own fault; he was 23 years old and was still living at home and putting up with the old man's bullshit. It was time for it to end. He looked over at his mother as she drove silently back to Burbank, evidently caught up with her own thoughts.

The next morning, Tyler woke to a hand stroking his face. He opened his eyes to see his mother sitting on the bed, tears in her eyes.

"Hi, honey, how are you?" His mother asked, wiping tears from her eyes and trying to smile. Tyler sat up in the bed and hugged her, saying nothing.

"I made breakfast for you,?" she asked anxiously. "Are you hungry?"

"Sure, Mom. Let me get dressed and I'll be right down."

Jill Taylor got up from the bed and reluctantly headed down to the kitchen. She wanted to hold her only child a little longer.

As he dressed, Tyler suppressed the urge to remain upset with his mother. He wanted to have a good visit with her, reminding himself that ,it might be the last time. He made his way downstairs and joined her at the kitchen table where she was sipping her coffee.

"You've lost even more weight since basic, honey," she said, surveying her son in shorts and a t-shirt.

"Yeah, I guess I have, mom," Tyler said. "The airborne training was very physical, not to mention the heat and humidity in Georgia. I don't need the weight anymore, you know, not playing football."

Tyler wasn't sure how to talk with her. It was awkward, even if she was his mother.

"So are you still with Danny?" Tyler asked, already knowing the answer.

"I am, Tyler, but let's not talk about him. I want to talk about us and our relationship, about your frightful journey to that hellhole. I am so afraid, Tyler."

His mother started to cry again and walked over to hug him. Tyler held onto her for a long time.

"I'll be fine, Mom," he said. "I've gotten a lot of training and I am going to be with the best."

"Tyler, that war is so wrong. It's a big lie being told by LBJ and his lackeys. Can't you see that?"

"Even if I did agree with you, Mom, I would still have to go. I really need to do this, not only for my country but for me. Maybe you can't see it, but I am changing, hopefully into a better man."

They spent the morning together. His mother looked so young that anyone seeing them walking along the beach might have thought they were a couple. She had arranged to stay with Tyler and his dad for a week before returning to Big Sur. That had to be hard on his dad, Tyler thought. He couldn't understand, why just once, he didn't unload on her. He never did. He really was a gentleman; gentle being the operative word.

Later that afternoon, Tyler drove the short distance to Patty's house. He rang the doorbell and nervously waited until Mrs. Olsen opened the door.

"Oh, Tyler, how are you?"she said, obviously surprised.

"I was wondering if Patty was here, Mrs. Olsen."

"Yes, she is, Tyler. Would you like to come in?"

Tyler was led into the living room where Patty sat on the sofa reading a magazine. She jumped up upon seeing him.

"Tyler, what are you doing here?" she asked, giving him a sisterly hug that her mother watched closely.

"I'm home on leave Patty. I am being sent to Vietnam in a couple weeks."

Patty frowned and asked him to sit down, motioning to a chair across from the couch. Her mother joined her on the couch, making it obvious to Tyler she wasn't about to leave them alone. He told her about his training to be a medic and completing the requirements for his airborne wings. She filled him in on her husband Sam's training. He was learning to be a clerk-typist at Fort Carson in Colorado. She didn't think he would have to go to Nam. Tyler only nodded to that bit of news. What he really wanted to do was talk to her privately, not with her mother hanging on every word. The tension in the room was getting unbearable and he finally said he had better get going.

She followed him outside to his Woody. Her mom stayed inside the house after he said goodbye.

"I want you to know I've thought a lot about us recently," Tyler said when they reached the car. She started to say something and he stopped her.

"Just let me finish, Patty," he said. "I know you're married, but I have to tell you something. It took me a long time to realize that I will always love you. I should have known it a long time ago, but I was an idiot. I don't know what life holds for us. Maybe this will be the last time I see you or maybe we will be together in the future. God only knows. I just wanted you to know you were right about everything and I was so wrong."

He reached for the door handle and started to turn away from her when she took his hand and pulled him to her. She touched the side of his face and kissed him lightly on the cheek.

"Tyler, I waited so long for you to say those words, now they are almost meaningless. Why oh why did you wait so long?" Tears were streaming down her cheeks when she turned back toward the house. Tyler watched her walk out of his life for the second time.

He sat in the Woody, not quite knowing what to do next. He decided to drive over to Petrov's to see if he wanted to get a beer. Tyler didn't want to drink alone. Maybe a beer would make the ache in his stomach go away, but he was sure it wouldn't help his heart.

Mike Petrov was lying by the pool when Tyler arrived. He introduced Tyler to his parents then grabbed them both a beer. He thought Tyler looked like hell.

"So what's up? Why so glum?" he asked.

Tyler explained his meeting with Patty, but left out a lot of the details. He wasn't much for sharing his deepest thoughts.

"That sounds like a great way to start our leave," Petrov said. "You need to get your mind off that girl. We need to find some women. I am getting tired of living like a monk. Let's get out of Newport and head inland. Maybe we can find some ladies who don't have coke bottles stuck up their asses."

Petrov had been put down by too many rich Newport Beach girls, Tyler thought. Before Tyler could answer, Mike's father Nick walked out and joined them.

"So Vietnam for you too, huh, Tyler? The way Mike just lays around the pool and spends my money, I am hoping some V.C. is a good shot. You don't take advantage of your parent's do you, Tyler?"

Tyler couldn't believe what he just heard Mr. Petrov say. He sat there stunned.

"Why don't you go drown yourself old man?" Mike said, standing up and towering over his much shorter father.

"No reason to get excited, son," his father said quickly. "I was just kidding, but you can start buying your own beer."

Mr. Petrov retreated into the house, leaving a flushed Mike staring at his heels. "See why I like being home?"

"Jesus," was all Tyler could utter.

They never did find any of the "inland" girls that Petrov fantasized about, well at least not anyone Tyler wanted to be seen with. They ended up drinking beer at the Pussycat -- the latest all nude bar to open in Santa Ana. The dancer, a young Mexican girl, gyrated on a circular stage he and Petrov sat at with about four other horny young men. It wasn't Tyler's idea of a great time, but at least he was doing something besides thinking of Patty.

"So do you think I can crash at your place tonight?" a down and out Petrov asked him, still stinging from his father's comment.

"Not tonight, Mike," Tyler said. "Remember my mom's there and it's already too confusing."

"Right, I forgot you have your own little hell."

Petrov was on his fifth beer and third bourbon chaser and was starting to slur his words. "Shake them honey," he yelled at the dancer ,who obliged by shaking her breasts in his face.

"Hey, Mike, let's get out of here," Tyler said. "I know a place in Newport we can go. You'll have fun. "

He noticed Petrov no longer was smiling. In fact, for no reason, he was glaring at a long-haired guy sitting across from them. Tyler knew the look. He was guilty of giving it a hundred times himself. Petrov didn't need a fight in the shape he was in, even if the Mr. Longhair tried his best to avoid looking back at Petrov.

Tyler pulled Petrov up from the table and threw down a twenty to cover the drinks. "You're going to have to settle for beach girls, Mike," Tyler said as they walked out into the night. He felt better in the Woody as they drove back to Newport with the windows down. Petrov was asleep before they traveled five miles.

CHAPTER 17

The Oregon/USC game wasn't even close. USC ran its tailback offense until the Oregon defense was exhausted. Tyler, for the first time, sat in the stands with his father. His old friend, Dean Whitman, the defensive tackle for the Trojans had scored him some seats just behind the home team Tyler had played for not so long ago.

"Must feel a little odd to be sitting in the stands," Tyler's father had commented at halftime as they snacked on hotdogs. They were in the Los Angeles Memorial Coliseum adjacent to the campus of USC. The stadium could hold up to 93,000 people. There were far less than that today, Tyler noted as he looked around the massive oval.

He did feel funny not be able to contribute anything more than cheering for his team. He longed to be able to hit someone or cover a pass. "Jesus, I really screwed up a big opportunity," he thought.

At the end of the lopsided SC victory he walked down on the field to congratulate his former team members. As he walked through them, someone touched him on the shoulder. He turned and was surprised to see Coach McKay.

"Tyler, I hear you're in the Army," McKay said. "How is it going?"

"Hi, coach. It's going OK, I guess. I am heading to Vietnam in less than a week. I would rather be out here playing for you. I am really sorry for what happened."

"Well we could use you, Tyler. You look like you're in great shape, son. When you get back, why don't you come and see me. Maybe you will be ready to play some ball and be a student again."

Tyler beamed as his dad walked up and put his arm around his son and exchanged greetings with Coach McKay. The entire encounter was maybe only a minute, but Tyler thought it might have been one of the most meaningful conversations of his life. Maybe he had a chance to play Pac-10 football again.

He was still walking around and greeting his former friends when he saw Coach Dewitt talking with a reporter on the sidelines. He was the quarterback coach Tyler had punched, which ultimately led to his dismissal.

"Dad, I need to talk to someone. I'll catch up with you at the car."

Tyler didn't want to drag his dad along for this conversation. He waited patiently by the SC bench, waiting for Dewitt to finish his interview before approaching him. Most of the players had left the field for the locker room by the time Tyler walked up to the young quarterback coach.

"Coach, could I talk with you for a minute?"

Dewitt turned and looked surprised to see Tyler Taylor. "What is it Taylor? I thought you were in the Army."

"I am, coach. I am home on leave for a couple weeks before I ship out for Nam. I just wanted you to know how sorry I am for hitting you. Believe me, I have regretted doing so ever since it happen. I don't expect you to forgive me; I just needed to tell you that."

Coach Dewitt could see real remorse in Taylor's eyes, but it was hard not to remember how miserable he was with a wired jaw. It was still painful, even now.

"Well, Tyler, I do appreciate you saying so. I am sorry to hear you are going to Vietnam and I wish you well."

Dewitt shook his hand and ran off towards the locker room, leaving Tyler standing at the empty team bench. "I don't blame him if he's still mad," Tyler thought. "At least I finally apologized."

Tyler couldn't contain his excitement when he met his dad back at the parking lot.

"I want to come back here, dad when I finish my tour with the Army," he said. "I think I might have the chance to start over, maybe do it right this time."

His dad embraced him. "You can do it, Tyler. Just take care of yourself over there. This will all work out for you. I have seen a real change in you since you've been in the Army. We all have to grow up and face our past demons, son. You're no different."

"How about your demons, dad?" Tyler said, abruptly changing the subject. "How will you go on without mom? I worry about you too."

Tyler held his dad at arm's length, carefully studying his reaction.

"Tyler, I can't change your mother. I have to move on with my life and she with her's. Just always know we both love you and always will."

They drove silently back to Newport Beach. Tyler contemplated the mix of feelings he had experienced in the last few days. It reinforced his desire to forgive and move on with his life. That meant his mom too, he told himself. He wanted to leave here with a clean conscience and love, not hate, in his heart. Maybe he would even forgive himself.

The sun was barely visible in the morning fog as it rose to illuminate the Pacific Ocean. Tyler sat on the beach staring at the blue gray water off Newport Beach. He had risen early on his last day here. Today he would leave for the Oakland Army Base and his eventual flight to Southeast Asia and the small country of Vietnam. He pondered the fact he may never see this place again.

The fighting had become intense from all accounts he read and the endless coverage on TV was frightening. He had read several accounts of the 173rd battles in the Central Highland cities of Dak To and Kontum. He figured that's where he and Raab would he heading too.

He had to admit it scared him. As he prepared to leave the beach, he filled a small glass vial with some sand and sealed it with a cork stopper. At least he would have a little bit of home with him, he thought.

He had spent the night before talking at length with his mom. It was a tearful and meaningful experience. He told her he loved her and forgave her. She looked relieved and happy when they finally went to bed. She was still sleeping when he entered her bedroom to say goodbye. She hugged him with all her strength.

"I will pray for you every day, Tyler," she said.

It was all she managed to say before he left her and joined his father in the garage. His Woody was parked next to his dad's Buick. He stared at it for a long minute. It was like looking back on his youth.

"I'll take care of it for you, son," his dad said as he loaded Tyler's duffel bag into the trunk. "It will be here for you when you return."

Petrov was getting a ride with them to the airport where they would hook up with Raab for the flight to San Francisco. After picking up Petrov they rode in silence to LAX. There was really nothing else to say, Tyler thought.

"Look, I want to see Carol."

Petrov was still whining after they all checked in at the Oakland Army Base and were told they were restricted to base until their flight left for Vietnam. It had been his plan to see the famous stripper Carol Doda before they departed, and he wanted Taylor and Raab with him.

"She has the most famous jugs in the country and we're only a few miles away from seeing them," he said. "We can get out of here. No one will miss us."

Petrov kept it up for almost an hour before Raab and Taylor finally gave in.

They made a hasty exit through the barracks window and caught a cab outside the base. The driver knew right where to go. "She's in North Beach at the Condor Club. Did you know she has 44 D breasts?" He asked Petrov as they drove towards San Francisco.

"I know all about her," he responded, smiling back at his two buddies who were sitting in the back seat.

"Do you know about the initials A.W.O.L, Mike?" Raab asked, returning the grin.

"What the fuck! Maybe we'll be sent to Vietnam. Hey at least we'll be together."

Tyler knew that Petrov was still smarting about being assigned to the 25th.

They ordered overpriced beer and waited for the show to begin. The bar was packed with businessmen, soldiers, street people and hippies, almost all of them male. The music began and Carol Doda was slowly lowered from the ceiling on a grand piano that she was dancing on top of. She performed in a topless bathing suit. The three young soldiers sat transfixed as they watched the show.

"My God, those are the biggest knockers I've ever seen," Petrov whispered as if he were in church.

Tyler's thoughts drifted back to his leave and the goodbyes just said. He wasn't that interested in Carol Doda. It was odd, but now he was anxious to get going. This stuff was going to be all in the past. After her second show, which Petrov insisted they stay for, the three friends made their way back to the barracks. Nobody even questioned why they were showing up at three in the morning.

The next afternoon Tyler and Raab were assigned a flight. Petrov was left behind as they boarded a bus to Travis Air Force base. Before leaving they made a pact to keep in touch with him as best they could.

Taylor and Raab boarded the MAC transport plane, finding the seats all faced towards the rear of the plane. Tyler had the thought that maybe they didn't want you to see where you were going. The plane made a refueling stop in Hawaii. The troops were not allowed out of a restricted area guarded by MPs, j in case somebody changed their mind about the trip. At least they had decent snacks and plenty of rest rooms.

The next stop was a refuel in the Marshal Islands. All Tyler and Raab could see was a lot of lava. A few hours after takeoff, the pilot advised them they needed to check the plane out in the Philippines. Evidently something was wrong with the braking system.

"Great, we probably won't even give the VC a chance to kill us," Raab said, frowning and slumping further into his seat. "We'll end up as scrap metal on some airfield."

The soldiers let out a loud cheer after the big plane finally managed to stop on the tarmac at Clark Air Force Base.

A master sergeant entered the plane at the terminal and walked to the rear of the it to address the somewhat nervous troops.

"OK, men, the repairs on your plane may take awhile," he said. "You will be billeted here at the base. You will be advised when to report back here for the last leg of your flight. You are restricted to the base, but you are welcome to use the bars at the NCO or EM clubs, depending on your rank. You will pick up your gear and follow me to the transport buses."

Tyler had always thought that Fort Benning had to be the hottest and most humid place on the planet; he was wrong. He stepped off the plane into a sauna. The humidity immediately drenched Tyler's shirt with sweat.

"Jesus, do you think it's this hot in Nam?" he asked Raab, who was pulling his duffel bag from the pile next to the plane. Raab looked up from his task and looked like a water hose had been turned on him. "I think the fun is just beginning Tyler."

They entered an equally hot bus and took a short ride to the transient barracks. After picking out their bunks for the night Tyler started stripping off his uniform.

"I need a shower," he said to Raab, who readily agreed to join him. They wrapped towels around them, donned flip-flops and headed out.

After about 20 minutes under tepid water, they headed back to the barracks. By the time both sat on their bunks they were covered in perspiration again. Neither bothered to dress and, fatigued from the flight, they fell asleep almost immediately. By the time they woke, it was early evening and the mess hall was closed for the night.

"Let's find a cold drink and something to eat. I am starved," Tyler said with a moan as they slipped back into their much wrinkled and not quite dry uniforms.

The NCO/EM club looked the same as every other one Tyler had been in. They took a seat at an empty table on the EM side of the club. Tyler ordered a beer and Raab a Coke. At least the place had air conditioning and the Filipino band wasn't bad. Tyler was on his third beer and beginning to relax when a young sergeant sat down at their table. Tyler recognized him from their plane.

"Headed to the Nam, huh?" he asked in a soft voice that didn't match his rough appearance. He was at least 6 foot, 3 and probably weighed at least 220 pounds. His hair was close cropped and his weary eyes looked like they had seen a lot, Tyler thought. He had two rows of combat ribbons, including a Silver Star, topped with a Combat Infantryman's badge and airborne wings. He wore the shoulder patch of the 173rd Airborne on his right sleeve.

Raab answered before Tyler could say anything.

"That's right, actually to your old unit," he said, nodding at the shoulder patch.

The young sergeant sighed and took a sip of his beer.

"What's your MOS?" he asked, finishing his beer in one final swig.

"We're medics, 91A10s," Raab replied. "How about you, Sarge?"

"I am a platoon sergeant. Going back for my second tour. I was part of the first deployment in '65. My name's Dave Jenner."

The big sergeant shook hands with Raab and Taylor, who both introduced themselves.

"So how is it there, Dave?" Tyler asked after ordering another round of beers for himself and Jenner.

"Well, I think it's going to be a lot tougher this time now that we're in the Central Highlands," Jenner said. "When I was there in '65 we were in Bien Hoa. We had been training in Okinawa. Lots of jumps and training before we got there. I was only 19 arid pretty gung ho.

We all thought we would go in and kick ass, then get out. Instead we started training in airmobile assaults. You'll see Nam is not very well suited for jumping into the action. You have to get in and then find a way to get out. Anyway we spent a couple months training before we saw any real action. I was sent to Kontum Province to help out the "Green Beanies" at their camps. Raab looked confused. Jenner understood. "Green Beanies", you know Special Forces. Raab nodded and Jenner continued. Anyway Charlie was evidently getting pissed about them being in the area. After that we ended up in Pleku, which by the way is where we're flying into, if we ever get out of here. Anyway I was fine until Operation Hump, after we hooked up with the 1st Division. By then we were back near Bien Hoa in what they refer to as the Iron Triangle. I was assigned to Charlie Company 1/503d and we walked into one hell of an ambush of automatic weapons fire. Our lead platoon got really shot up. We could have used you guys. Lots of shot troops. The damn jungle was so thick that mortars were useless. We were pinned down. The gooks were so close, the brass couldn't use artillery or air strikes. It went hand- to- hand fighting, grenades going off. We finally got some support from Alpha and Bravo companies. I got hit twice and got evaced to a rear aid station. A couple of guys like you saved my ass."

"Were you sent home?" a transfixed Tyler asked as Jenner went back to his beer.

"I eventually ended up in Japan for treatment of my wounds. After a month, I was sent back to Nam. I spent the rest of my tour at headquarters and never really got back into the jungle."

"Shit, Dave, how come you didn't get out? Wasn't your enlistment up?" Tyler asked, now gulping his beer down.

"I re-enlisted ,Tyler. I guess you would say I am a lifer. I actually like the Army and the action. I would add, however, that getting shot is no fun."

Tyler and Raab kept buying the beer and listened to Jenner's describe life in Vietnam.

They closed the club and Raab had to help both Tyler and Jenner back to the barracks. Both were pretty toasted.

The next morning they were notified that their aircraft was ready. They boarded and the plane took off heading east. Their next stop would be Pleku, Vietnam.

CHAPTER 18

"I thought I heard a young man morn this morning.
I thought I heard a young man morn today,
I thought I heard a young man morn this morning I
can't walk you out in the morning dew today."
"Morning Dew" by Bonnie Dobson

"Gentlemen, we have received mortar fire from the enemy when we have made this landing before. Be prepared to run for shelter if we encounter any," the stern MAC sergeant announced as they prepared to land in Pleku.

"I guess there won't be a little adjustment period to all this," Raab said as they looked out the window at a lot of green below them.

"Yeah, he also didn't mention where to run to," Tyler said, leaning across Raab to get a better look at their new home for the next year. It looks peaceful from up here, he thought.

It turned out they didn't have to run after landing. After picking up their duffel bags they followed Jenner to the replacement center. Both Taylor and Raab thought that sticking with Jenner would be a good idea.

When they finally arrived at the replacement company, Jenner took them aside.

"Listen, you guys will have to do a week of jungle training before they assign you to a unit. It's kind of joke because you won't learn much until you're in the bush. When you get there don't say much and try to learn quickly. A lot of seasoned troops won't give a new guy the time of day. They figure you won't be around long enough to matter. When you do get into the shit, try not to panic. Oh, the other thing to remember, don't let them yell "medic" at you when they need help. The gooks wait to see who moves and they try to take him out. Have them call you "doc" or your own name.

"Why do they try to kill the medics?" Tyler asked, starting to get nervous.

"They figure it will lower morale. Same thing for the lieutenants. They like to eliminate the leadership, too. Don't underestimate the little fuckers, they're smart. "

Jenner left the next morning for Dak To, leaving Taylor and Raab to complete their indoctrination program in Pleku. The makeshift camp had about 25 tents for the newly arrived soldiers. The food consisted of c-rations. Small boxes that contained a couple tin cans. One was the main dish and the other was usually fruit. It was just something to eat to keep you from starving.

After a week of training, they went on their first patrol with the other replacements just outside the base at Camp Enari.

It was a practice mission, but the advisers made it clear that there were no safe places in Vietnam. About 40 men who went outside the base just before the sun went down. The two master sergeants leading the patrol split the group in two. Taylor and Raab were the only medics, so the sergeants split them up. They carried medical aid packs and had familiarized themselves with the contents.

Tyler had been assigned to the group lead by Sergeant Woods. He was part of the 4th Divisions 1st Infantry training group. He pulled Tyler and the radio operator aside as they prepared to move out.

"You two stick close to me," he said, nodding at the radio man, "You right behind me and Taylor, you behind him."

After walking about a half mile, they entered the jungle. Tyler was amazed how much of the light was immediately lost to the canopy. They moved slowly behind the sergeant, the only sound was the occasional banging of equipment carried by the men. After about 300 yards, the sergeant spread the men out. He then took small groups further out from the group and set up Claymore antipersonnel mines. Prior to the mission, they learned the VC often would sneak in and turn the mines back towards the troops. White tape was now placed on the back of the mines so they could be seen by whoever was on guard duty. When detonated, the mines would spew 700 steel balls over a sixty-degree arc 50 meters in distance. Tyler never wanted to be in front of one when it was fired.

While some were setting the mines, the rest of the men were digging foxholes for the night. Tyler could only guess how many of these he would be digging in the future. It started raining just as they were settled in for a long night. He could hear the sound of artillery being fired in the distance. It sounded like far away thunder. He had not slept at all when he was told it was time for him to take over as the guard in his foxhole. He had been issued an M-16 rifle for the patrol. During his medical training the instructors had told them that most medics in Vietnam carried .45 caliber handguns for protection. Carrying an M-16 was impractical when you needed to treat injured soldiers in combat. Your first priority was to care for your men.

Tyler focused his vision on the white tape of the Claymore mine; half expecting an agile VC soldier sneaking up to turn it around on him. He tried to listen, but he could only hear the pounding of the heavy rain. His guard responsibility was for two hours, 0200 to 0400 hours. He finally looked away from the Claymore and saw that Sergeant Woods was watching him from the far end of the foxhole. He nodded in the affirmative and a small grin came across his face. Tyler didn't understand the significance of it, but smiled back.

About a mile away from Tyler's patrol, John Raab sat in another foxhole. He too was awake and silently praying. It dawned on him that to ever see home again he would have to survive 360 more nights like this. His logical mind told him the odds weren't very good. He had been hearing all the stories of the 173rd Sky Soldiers and the Battle of the Slopes, where a whole platoon was wiped out by the NVA, half of them executed after being wounded. The group he had walked out here with made so much noise, he was sure that any enemy soldiers in the area would have no problem pinpointing their location. Because of all the rain, he strained to see through his wet glasses. He had nothing dry to wipe them off with. He would "make do" he told himself. Like Tyler, he had been assigned to the foxhole with the sergeant leading the patrol. It made him feel a little better that someone with experience was with him. For now, at least, all was quiet.

The next morning at first light, the foxholes were filled and the two patrols joined up near the west end of Camp Enari. After returning to the replacement company, Raab, Taylor and the other 173rd soldiers were transported to Bien Hoa for assignment. The 173rd Support Battalion was there.

Captain Anderson gave them their orders.

"Taylor, you got the plum assignment. You're going to the 2/503rd at Dak To," he said. "Those guys have been through hell lately. We are now going to be permanently in the Central Highlands, II Corps zone. This base is being moved to An Khe most ricky tic. Raab you're going to the 4/503rd. For now you'll be at Tuy Hoa, on the coast regrouping. Enjoy the surf?"

"Sir, I am the one who surfs, not Raab," Tyler said, trying to add a little humor to the moment.

"Oh I know who you are, Taylor. I went to SC and read all about you getting kicked off the team," Anderson replied. "I take it you're not too bright, giving that all up."

Tyler was stunned. It was the first time since basic that anyone knew about his problems at college.

"Yes, sir, I wasn't too bright; in light of where I am right now."

"Well, Taylor, you'll have plenty of opportunities for fights here," the captain said. "The problem is the other guys have guns and bombs too."

After leaving the captain's office they sat at the mess hall eating lunch.

"Shit, what are the chances of running into somebody from USC?" Tyler moaned, looking at a cup of soup and baloney sandwich in front of him. "I thought all the grads there found a way of staying out of the military; unless they went into the Navy. He probably went out of his way to get me the "plum" assignment to the 2/503rd... Don't you just love the Army, John."

"Tyler, I have to tell you after last night in the jungle, I can't imagine surviving a year here," Raab said. "That's the negative. The weird thing was I felt like I belonged out there."

It didn't take Tyler very long to find out how he would do in the jungle. He had no sooner arrived at the 2/503rd when got his first assignment.

"OK, Taylor, I want you to pay attention. We keep losing medics and I don't like it one bit. I want you to stick close to me and listen when I tell you to do something. It could save your sorry ass."

Tyler was listening to Sergeant McClug, who would be leading his first mission. It was an ambush patrol consisting of seven soldiers and one medic. They were preparing to poke around in the Tumuroung Valley just north of Dak To. It was part of something the Army was calling Task Force 77 and they were looking for NVA.

"We move slowly through the jungle, stop and listen. Watch where you put your feet down, lots of booby traps. The helicopter will drop us off at dusk. We'll hump until its dark, then set-up. After awhile we'll move again very quietly and set up again for the night just in case the gooks get a look at us. Taylor, these guys are like ghosts in the jungle; never underestimate them. I want you right behind the RDO and remember to keep your spacing."

Tyler had learned that McClug was on his second tour and had previously been with 5th Special Forces. He was happy to be going out with an experienced sergeant and team of Sky Soldiers. He was told to pack lightly, but still had about 50 pounds of medical equipment to carry. McClug had him cut it in half. They all wore soft headgear. There wouldn't be any foxholes tonight, he figured.

Tyler donned his Australian bush hat and Navy fowl weather parka, both of which he had brought from home. He boarded the Huey helicopter at the Dak To airstrip and headed north. They flew very low over the jungle canopy. The rotors of the helicopter making the only sound he could hear. The helicopter dropped to about 15 feet off the ground when McClug ordered them to jump. As he hit the ground, his pack shifted forward and he ended up falling face first into the mud. Without a word, McClug pulled him to his feet. He motioned towards the point man, who was already moving out. Within minutes the jungle engulfed them and Tyler was finding it hard to see the radio operator in front of him.

He finally realized it was easier to follow the whipping antenna silhouetted in the subdued fading light. As they moved slowly through the jungle, Tyler finally got his breathing back to normal. As McClug promised, there were many stops and they would squat down listening to the quiet sounds of the jungle.

Their final stop was halfway up the side of a hill overlooking a trail. You could barely see it, though, from their position some 100 yards above it. About the time they settled into their ambush positions, the rains came. McClug crawled up beside him.

"If you can, get a little shut-eye," he said. "You have guard duty at 0300 until we move out at 0500. I'll wake you."

Tyler lay back against the tree he was hiding behind. He didn't think he slept until the sergeant shook him.

"OK, Taylor, I'll be right above you. If you see anything, wake me first before you start shooting. "

McClug moved away into the darkness and Taylor sat up staring at the trail. He looked down at the .45 strapped into a shoulder holster under his left arm. I am sure not going to attack any VC with that, he thought to himself.

It was cool here in the mountains and he was thankful he had the parka on. He had just shifted his position to get a better view of the trail when he thought he saw a man move quickly up the trail. Tyler wondered if his mind was playing tricks on him. It happened so fast he just wasn't sure with all the rain and poor visibility. He was still pondering what to do when the man ran back again towards where he had come from. Tyler moved just as quick to Sergeant McClug, shaking him awake and quietly telling him what he had seen. The rest of the patrol were awakened and took up defensive positions. McClug and Tyler crab-walked back to the large tree Tyler had seen the man from.

"The VC always sends out a point man to clear the trail for the rest. His friends should be along shortly. We want to see how many there are before we do anything," McClug whispered, handing Tyler an M-79 grenade launcher and a bandolier of ammo.

"Know how to use this?" Tyler shook his head in the negative.

"Just like a shotgun, sort of. Just point and shoot. We don't have time for instructions right now."

McClug then moved along to the other men, whispering instructions.

About 10 long minutes later a small squad of men began to move in front of their position. All of a sudden the ridge side erupted with gunfire. Tyler fired the M-79 at the last place he had seen the men on the trail. Then, in a matter of seconds, several bodies were on the ground; the rest had disappeared into the jungle and were returning fire at the patrol. Tyler had just reloaded the weapon when McClug ran up to his position.

"We're getting out of here, Taylor. Grab your stuff and follow me."

The patrol moved out up the hill while the VC scrambled around below them, continuing to fire in their direction. Tyler ran behind the agile sergeant, who had at least 10 years on him. The adrenalin surged through his body and he had little trouble keeping up. He could hear the rest of the patrol as they made their way up to the top of the hill.

As they crested the top, McClug stopped them. Tyler could hear only heavy breathing at first; his own. "They're behind us, move out in single file," McClug said.

For the next two hours, they moved across the hills, staying on the high ground. Tyler imaged the VC following just behind them. It was first light when they came down into a flat valley and waited in the jungle for a helicopter to take them out.

"It's going to be about 20 minutes before our pick-up," McClug explained to the very tired men gathered around him. He assigned two men to backtrack a couple hundred meters to protect the rear. He was confident the VC were no longer following, but was taking no chances.

Tyler caught his breath and leaned against a tree. He was still carrying the M-79.

He couldn't believe his first mission had resulted in contact with the enemy. He had been briefed, when he reported in to his company, that most patrols had seen a lot of NVA signs, but contact had been negligible. Now they had something to report.

He watched as McClug grabbed the radio from the RDO. He spoke quietly to the pilot of the Huey, giving their location for extraction. A red smoke grenade was thrown out and soon Tyler heard the helicopter approach the clearing. As soon as it landed, the patrol ran to board it. McClug waited for the two men he had sent back. When he had gathered them up, they all ran to the Huey and jumped on board. It was quiet in the "bird" as the men flew back to Dak To.

After landing, McClug walked off the tarmac with Tyler.

"Taylor, you handled yourself well out there," he said. "A lot of guys panic their first time in combat. You did fine. Get some chow and sleep."

Tyler dropped his gear off at the medics' tent and joined the rest of the patrol at the mess hall. The cooks were serving undercooked bacon and watery eggs, He didn't care; he was starved.

"You did good, Doc," Corporal Terry Gates, the radio operator on the patrol, said as he sat down across from Tyler.

It was the first time anyone had called him doc, Tyler thought. It was of course what most of the medics were called by soldiers throughout Vietnam. It still sounded special to Tyler, who grinned at the radio operator.

The rest of the patrol gathered at the table and began critiquing the mission.

"You know McClug's got it right," a private named Welsh said. "Hit the damn VC just like they ambush us. The man know how to fight this war."

Tyler had learned Welsh was from Detroit. He was a large black guy who had played football in high school before joining the Army. He was nineteen years old and looked thirty. He went on with his speech, not addressing it to anyone in particular. "Asshole generals want to set out whole companies just to get shot up. Small units, that's the ticket. Hit and run."

Welsh looked over at Tyler.

"So how long you got to go there, Doc? Over 300 and a wake-up? Shit I'd kill myself if I had that long to go."

Tyler grinned and pointed his finger to his head in a mock suicide.

"Oh, better not kill yourself yet, Doc. I still got a hundred days or so. You might have to patch me up yet."

That night Tyler stared through the mosquito net that hung above his cot. The mesh distorted his view of the tents ceiling. Distorted he thought. That's how the firefight had felt. Did he actually kill another human being? He couldn't be sure. At the time, he didn't even think about it. It was all reaction. Still it took him a long time to go to sleep.

CHAPTER 19

Mike Petrov slapped the back of his neck and killed the first red fire ant to bite him that day. It wouldn't be the last. He was awake from what he now called sleep. It was more like a distressed nap. It was time to rejoin his Infantry platoon after a night on ambush patrol. He watched as the seven soldiers he had spent the night with started to move out quietly through the jungle that was now his home.

The 25th Infantry, his new unit, was based in Cu Chi. He had arrived there after flying to Saigon. After being assigned to the 1st Battalion, 25th Infantry Division, he spent several weeks learning the ropes at the Battalion aide station. Most of the medics there were either new or getting ready to rotate home. It came as no surprise when he was assigned to the field. He joined a platoon in the Iron Triangle, immediately replacing a medic who was going home.

The medic had some advice for him.

"Listen Petrov, everything is fucked up out there," he said. "The floor of that jungle is death. You have snakes, ants, leaches, punji sticks, mines. Well you get the picture. You spend your day listening to the troops bellyache about anything that might get them out of the field. Your job is to keep them out there. You'll need all of them if you run into Mr. Charles."

"Who's Mr.Charles?" Petrov asked.

"Shit, Petrov! Charlie, VC, the fucking enemy. Didn't they teach you anything at your airborne school?"

"Just how to jump out of planes," Petrov said, sneering. He didn't like this guy. He was wishing he had been assigned to the 173rd with Raab and Taylor.

"Well if the jungle doesn't kill you, the VC will sure in the hell try to."

Petrov was learning. Nobody cared much about you when you were new. His only redeeming quality was that he was a medic. The bastards never knew when they might need him.

After a month in the field he had seen no action. He had, however, become proficient in digging bunkers. The drill had become endless days of walking through the jungle looking for the miles of tunnels dug by the enemy and, of course, the enemy himself. Nights found him inside a bunker, joining small ambush patrols or, his favorite, the listening post assignment. The LP found you alone in the jungle hundreds -- if not thousands -- of meters from your company with a radio. You spent the night hoping you didn't hear the VC trying to sneak up on you. If you heard them coming, you were supposed to call the patrol. Of course that meant they would soon be firing in your direction. Nobody had told him what in the hell he was supposed to do in the meantime. The problem with all these assignments was that you never got to sleep. When you came back in the morning, it was time to move out again.

He had just started his sixth week in the jungle when his unit, with no explanation, was flown back to the base camp for a break. After a shower and change into a clean uniform, he read the mail that was waiting there for him. The first letter he opened was from Raab.

Dear Mike,

I hope you are having as much fun as I am. If I had known what a ball Vietnam would be, I would have signed up sooner. Actually it did start out pretty good for me. The unit I was assigned to was recovering on the coast after getting their ass kicked at Dak To.

So I was sent to a place called Tuy Hoa. I have been enjoying the beach, beer and nurses. Well maybe not the latter. Tyler got screwed and went to Dak To or Kontum. He wasn't sure when he left. Either place is a hell hole. I heard it's flat where you are. It's all hills and mountains here. Makes humping real fun.

Since being in Tuy Hoa and we had a barbecue on the beach. Is this making you jealous? We do actually have missions. I went out with Alpha Company in search of the elusive VC. They don't think the NVA are around here like in the Central Highlands. We have been told we are looking for VC guerrilla units, which translates to farmers who fight at night and tend their crops during the day. I got into my first fight last week and patched up my first casualty. We were in the cost mountain region of Phu Yen on an ambush patrol. Our scout unit located a small group of VC in a clearing about a mile from our location. The captain had us deploy around the VC who were apparently sleeping. After a short firefight, most of the VC were wiped out. A grenade was thrown by one of our guys and the shrapnel caught another Sky Soldier across the way in the bush. The result was a nasty leg injury. I got to clean it up, pump him full of morphine and completed my first dust off. I looked at one of the VC they found alive. He had a sucking chest wound and by the time I started working on him, he died. Better them than us I thought. Anyway the gung ho captain we have told me he was putting me in for my Combat Medical Badge. He was all stoked he had finally killed some VC. I have a feeling that this is nothing compared to what we'll eventually see. The older sergeants all say we're heading back to Dak To -- soon. They all say its "bad shit" there. I hope Tyler's doing OK. As of this letter, I haven't heard from him. Hope all is well, Mike. Keep in touch when you can.

John

Petrov read the letter again before putting it in his rucksack. He smiled thinking about Raab. The rest of the letters were from his mother. Most were about the everyday things she did, nothing about his father. That was fine with him. He just wished the old bastard was out here humping the jungle with him. He wrote back to Raab and sent a letter to Tyler. He also hoped nothing had happen to his friend. Two days later Petrov headed back to the field, this time in a truck, packed in like sardines with the other troops. He looked out at the small villages and the people who lived in them. It was so different from Newport Beach and the life he had lived there. Most of the Vietnamese avoided making eye contact with the soldiers. Only the kids, who begged for food, reaching out towards them with extended hands, seemed unafraid of the army from the West. He had read their history. They had been at war for at least a hundred years. This was nothing new for them. They knew nothing else. The trucks continued north, back into the jungle.

CHAPTER 20

Sergeant Erin Smith halted his Long Range Reconnaissance Patrol, or LRRPs, on a hilltop just north of Dak To. He looked down into the valley before them. Something just didn't seem right. to him. He knew the NVA were out there somewhere and yet in two days out in the jungle, he had only seen signs of them -- no bodies and no live enemies.

This was his second tour and while he was only 26 years old, he was considered one of the old guys. He had learned on his previous tour to listen to that little voice inside his head that told him something was wrong. The valley could be a perfect ambush point if his small patrol had been observed. During his first tour he had walked into one of the NVA's famous horseshoe ambushes. Half of his company had been lost that day. This location looked eerily similar. For now they would just observe. It was a quiet two hours, as the prone soldiers scanned the valley.

It was just at dusk when Smith saw the faint light on the hill across the valley from where they lay. Someone was up there. He tapped his RDO on the shoulder, motioning him back to a large depression in the jungle where it was safe to call in artillery on the hill where he had observed the light. If the NVA where there, as he suspected, he would know in short order.

Soon, artillery lit up the now darkening skies as Smith crawled back to the hilltop and adjusted the fire. As the barrage tore up large chunks of jungle vegetation, he watched the unmistakable movement of men fleeing up the hill, trying to escape the nightmare he had brought down on them. It amazed him when they started to disappear, as if swallowed up by the earth. His veteran's mind knew the answer: tunnels, lots of them. Sgt. Smith didn't know it at the time, but the hill he was directing fire on -- Hill 875 -- would be the scene of one of the bloodiest battles of the Vietnam War. For now he just wanted to get his team out before the NVA discovered them. They moved out in the darkness, back the way they had come.

SP/4 Tyler Taylor woke to total darkness, his stomach churning. He thought he would throw up. He was soaked from his own sweat, even though the night was cool. He sat straight up and realized he was still in the forward firebase at Dak To, not in the jungle he had dreamed. He slept in his jungle fatigue pants, boots and a T-shirt on a cot covered with mosquito net. He pulled aside the net and stepped out of the tent into the dark night. There was no light, so the NVA couldn't zero in their rockets from the nearby hills. As his head cleared, he was able to suppress the need he had to vomit.

"Jesus," he thought. "I never had nightmares that vivid before. Too many stories from the veterans."

Tyler did some sit-ups, followed by 50 push-ups. He felt better and walked over to the mess tent in search of some coffee. Just after dawn a LRRP team came in from the field, searching for something to eat. He listened quietly as they sat across for him, debriefing their mission. From what he heard, it sounded like they had found a hill with a lot of gooks.

Later that morning the LRRP's findings translated into a mission for the 2/503rd. Tyler was going back into the jungle.

"Men, the NVA are dug in on Hill 875," Captain Mendoza told

the soldiers of Charlie Company. "We are not going to leave them there for long."

Tyler and the other soldiers soon boarded the Huey helicopters that would take them in close to the action they expected. They were joined by Delta Company near the base of Hill 875.

Tyler looked up the hill and sighed. It had heavy jungle cover with the exception of the areas blown away by the heavy artillery. Alpha company had been left behind at the landing zone. This would be their resupply point and medivac for the wounded.

The companies were within a couple hundred yards of the summit when they were hit with sniper and motor fire. A young paratrooper ahead of Tyler cried out he was wounded. As the fire intensified all around them, Tyler crawled forward to check on the wounded rifleman. As he neared him, he recognized it was Private Howland, who had been on the ambush patrol with him.

"I am hurting, Doc, help me." Howland implored Tyler as he reached his side.

A sniper's bullet had hit Howland's right leg and shattered the femur. The large bone was exposed and arterial blood flowed from the wound onto the jungle carpet.

"OK, man, we're going to get that bleeding stopped," Tyler said, turning the young man onto his back while pulling a tourniquet from his aid bag. He secured it above the wound and tightened it until the bleeding slowed.

Just then, a mortar exploded in front of their position. More men were calling out for help. Tyler placed a large compress dressing on the wound and again tied it tightly. He carried his morphine in his shirt pocket. His hands were shaking badly as he tried to remove one of the single shot doses from the cardboard packet and dropped it. He retrieved the packet and managed to administer the pain relieving drug to Howland.

"Hang in there Howland," he screamed. "We'll get you down the hill soon. Just don't move."

Tyler could hear intense M-60 machine gun fire off to his right and caught a glimpse of NVA soldiers moving down the hill towards them. He rushed to other wounded soldiers. He found a Sky Soldier just ahead of his last position. He was too late for him. Most of his face was missing when Tyler turned him over.

The wounded were everywhere and Tyler ran between them, helping those who were still alive, when he reached them. Most could still fight on, and it was evident to all that they were in the fight of their lives.

An hour into the fight Tyler returned to Howland to loosen his tourniquet. He found him in deep shock. He was able to start an saline solution IV after several attempts to find a vein. He injected another shot of morphine and changed the now blood soaked compress. After treating him, Tyler dragged the wounded soldier down the hill, where the American troops were hanging on to a piece of jungle. There was little water, but Tyler managed to get some for Howland. He would die or at a minimum lose the leg if he didn't get him medivaced. He left Holland in search of Captain Mendoza. He found him with the RDO in a bombed out crater behind a large tree.

"Listen, Doc, we are cut off from support," the captain said. "This damn jungle isn't helping with air support. I am trying to get what we can. Alpha company got hit trying to join up with us. What I am telling you is we can't get back to the LZ. You'll have to make do with what you have for now."

Mendoza was streaked with mud and blood. He figured the husky Mexican-American was maybe 30 years old. Since the fight started , he looked like he had aged 10 years.

"Plan on spending the night here, Doc," Mendoza shouted. "We'll move down as many wounded as we can."

The fighting was still intense as Tyler made his way back up the hill. He was about 50 feet from where he had left Mendoza when the ground in front of him erupted. He felt his body rise from the ground and fall back down the hill.

When he woke, he was covered in dirt and debris. His right forearm was ripped open and blood flowed from a jagged cut. He suspected the arm was broken, but he was still able to move it. He checked the rest of his body and was surprised to find he was in one piece. His neck was burning and he reached up and pulled a hot piece of shrapnel from it. Blood flowed from the wound. Tyler pulled out a compress and placed it on the source of the bleeding. He tied the loose ends of the compress around his neck to secure it. He made out a huge crater 100 yards up the hill. Whatever had blown up had to be huge, Tyler thought. He felt a hand pulling him back and turned to find Captain Mendoza. He had a crazed look and was screaming something. It dawned on Tyler he couldn't hear anything.

With Mendoza pulling him and somehow pushing with his legs he made it up to the crater. Mendoza was still screaming something.

"Jesus Doc, are you OK?" Tyler's head was beginning to clear a little. He nodded in the affirmative.

"Son of a bitch, now our own bastards are bombing us," Mendoza screamed, looking towards the sky and throwing up one hand in disgust.

One of the other medics patched up his arm and Tyler was glad to find that everything else seemed to work. The bleeding had stopped from the neck wound. He later learned one of our own planes had dropped a 500 pound bomb that missed its target and killed 20 of our own.

Tyler sat in the crater for over an hour as the fighting continued all around him. The NVA made a charge down the hill just before sunset. He had picked up an M -16 that was of no further use to a fallen paratrooper. Trying to patch someone up during this attack would be suicide. Right now Tyler was a rifleman trying to stay alive.

He moved up the hill by inches with his buddies. Bodies from both sides were everywhere. It was funny, but a calm came over him. He knew he would probably die and for some reason he lost his fear of death.

He focused on the hill in front of him and methodically picked out

NVA. He fired single shots instead of just spraying bullets. He watched as four NVA fell in front of him. He reloaded with another clip and was starting to fire again when a soldier off to his side cried out for help.

The medic part took over again. He was no longer the linebacker knocking down running backs or the soldier killing the enemy. His job was to help and the anger he felt slowly dissipated. He crawled over to the wounded man, but kept the M-16. The young soldier had a head and chest wound. A round had entered his helmet and spun around inside, causing mostly superficial damage with lots of bleeding. Tyler got the bleeding controlled with two compresses.

The chest wound was far more difficult. Shrapnel had penetrated the lung and Tyler was faced with a sucking chest wound. He used a piece of plastic wrapping from a compress dressing to seal the hole. He taped it to the soldier's chest and covered it with another compress he secured around his back. It was the best he could do. He rolled the man on side and found no exit wound.

Once again he dragged the soldier down through the now mutilated jungle canopy to the makeshift staging area for the wounded. Before leaving him, Tyler rechecked the dressing and started an IV, handing it to another wounded soldier to hold. He started back up the hill, but was stopped by Mendoza.

"Doc, you're one of the last medics still standing," the captain said. "You need to stay here with these men. It's almost dark and I don't think you can do much more up there until morning."

Tyler nodded and checked on the men before collapsing. on the ground. He realized he was exhausted. A soldier crawled over with another medical bag and handed it to him. "It was Doc Kendal's. He didn't make it."

Tyler took the bag and patted the soldier on his shoulder.

"Thanks," he said. "I am almost out of supplies. I'm really sorry about Kendal."

Tyler couldn't tell because of the darkness, but he was sure the soldier was crying as he crawled off.

There was nothing more he could do for the wounded. He was exhausted and he closed his eyes for a moment. He didn't know if he was praying or not, but he found himself asking for God's help.

He slept for no more than an hour, but still felt a little rested when he opened his eyes. It was quiet except for the moans of his wounded comrades.

The quiet didn't last very long. The artillery again started removing the top of Hill 875. The NVA weren't sitting still during the barrage. Just at dawn, they opened up on the remaining members of Tyler's company with RPG rounds. All hell broke out once again and Tyler watched in horror as Captain Mendoza fell to the ground. Tyler crawled up to help if he could. For Mendoza, there would be no help. Tyler found the captain who had saved him was now missing most of his head.

Tyler started thinking that nobody would survive this. They were almost out of food, water and ammunition. He had few medical supplies left and he had used all his morphine. Men cried out for help that they weren't going to receive.

Suddenly word came that reinforcements were on their way. The 4/503rd was coming. They might live after all.

Tyler helped move several of wounded men down to where the first helicopter was taking them out of hell. He was walking back to the other wounded when someone touched his shoulder from behind. Tyler turned to see Raab staring at what was left of him.

"Oh my God, Tyler! They told us all the medics had been killed."

Raab hugged his big friend ,who was covered in blood and mud. Tears began running down his cheeks.

He handed Tyler his canteen. Tyler drank deeply from it.

"John, can you help me?" Tyler asked. "I have a bunch of guys that need to be evacted. I am out of supplies."

Raab checked with his lieutenant and grabbed another medic and extra supplies. As they made their way up to the command post with Tyler, Raab was overwhelmed by all the bodies of fallen American soldiers. Body parts were everywhere. He forced back the urge to throw up and started praying silently to himself. This was insane, he told himself.

Tyler looked like death itself. His eyes were vacant. The handsome face, streaked with grimy blood, no longer looked like the confident jock Raab had known.

It wasn't until they started treating the other soldiers that Raab noticed Tyler was wounded.

"It's nothing compared to these guys," Tyler said, motioning at the 20 or so men lying on the ground.

"There are others who can help now," Raab said, gently leading his friend to a bombed out depression and sitting him down.

CHAPTER 21

The artillery and air support began the next assault on the hill. Raab watched from a foxhole as the bombs fell on the gloomy, dark hill. He thought of his parents and worthless brother who wanted to "kick ass" on the Viet Cong. Well, he thought, you should be here now and following me up this damn hill instead of rotting away in jail.

"Doc, I am so scared," Specialist 4th Class Ellsworth said, laying beside Raab in the foxhole waiting for the word to start up the hill. He was probably only 19 years old, just a kid.

"You'll be fine, Ellsworth," Raab reassured him. "Stick close to me. We'll get through this."

But he was feeling anything but confident. For one thing they lacked enough paratroopers to make a good run on the NVA. He wondered what idiot was calling the shots. Whoever it was, he obviously wasn't down here on the ground with the troops. Probably either in the air or in some secure Command Post, out of harm's way.

He surveyed what was left of the jungle in front of him. The trees were stripped of their branches. The ordnance from both sides had knocked most of the trees down to stumps. The hill was littered with equipment left from the dead and wounded. It looked like the dump he had gone to in L.A. with his dad. The smell in the air was death. The bodies were starting to rot. He wondered if God ever looked down on these scenes with disgust. We were his children, Raab thought. It must hurt him. He looked up at the sky, which was blue and clean.

He was still looking up when the NVA opened up with 60 and 82 mm mortars. Raab tried to dig himself deeper into the foxhole. Ellsworth was crying next to him. Raab place his arm around the shaken soldier until the barrage ended.

Cries for help were coming from the flank to Raab's left. He told Ellsworth to stay put and he headed out to help. He found Sergeant Haden holding in his guts, which were spilling out from a horrible stomach wound. Raab rolled him onto his back just as the enemy opened up with small-arms and automatic weapons fire. The rounds tore up the ground in front of him as he lay face down in the dirt. Soldiers off to his side returned the fire and he had time to place a large compression bandage on Haden, who had lost consciousness. Raab wrapped it tightly with rolled tape and yelled at Ellsworth to help him.

Ellsworth stood up, but was cut down by automatic weapons. He never had a chance.

Raab himself was pinned down again. This was bullshit he thought. He picked up Haden's M-16 and started firing back. He emptied the weapon. Somehow it calmed him. He threw the gun down and started pulling the sergeant back down the hill.

He finally got some help from one of the dug-in soldiers and managed to get Haden to the evacuation area. He left the critically wounded sergeant with two stretcher carriers and started back up the hill to check on Ellsworth, even though; he was sure he was dead.

Lieutenant Thorton intercepted him as he neared Ellsworth's foxhole.

"He's dead, Doc. I need you on the right flank. We have several wounded over there." The lieutenant pointed towards the fallen trees to his right.

"All right, sir," Raab answered the wide- eyed officer and started towards the wounded men.

He had only gone about 25 yards when an explosion behind him knocked him to the ground. A mortar round had fallen right where he had left the lieutenant. After pulling himself up he ran back to the lieutenant. The blast had taken his right leg off at the knee. Thorton stared down at his missing limb, screaming.

Raab knelt down and placed a tourniquet above the kneecap. There wasn't much blood, as the blast had seared the wound. He gave the lieutenant a shot of morphine, attached the empty syrette to his collar and bandaged his leg. The officer was also bleeding from shrapnel wound to his back. Raab stopped the bleeding with a compression bandage. The morphine was taking effect and Thornton had stopped screaming.

"You're going home, sir. Just keep telling yourself that."

As he pulled him back towards the evacuation area, he got help from another trooper, who helped him lift Thornton up and drag him to relative safety. As they lowered the wounded lieutenant to the ground, he pulled Raab down so he could hear his hoarse whisper.

"Doc, you have to help the others," he said. "They're my men."

"I'll get them, sir. Hang on. We'll get you out of here."

As Raab turned away, he thought, "This guy is a hero. Where are all the colonels and generals?" He moved back toward the hill. "The assholes. Easy for them to send men out to be maimed and die. "

As Raab made his way to the right flank, he realized nobody was moving up the hill. The Sky Soldiers were effectively pinned down. He passed one soldier behind a log, who yelled out at Raab.

"Hey, man, don't try to go anywhere. The gooks are all over the place. I think we lost 1st Platoon, man."

Raab ignored him and continued moving up to where he had last seen the downed soldiers. As he scrambled along the fallen trees he tripped over the body of one of them and went down hard. The dead soldier had saved his life. Just as he fell, a NVA B-40 rocket exploded ahead on the path he would have been on. A moment later he again heard the unmistakable swoosh of an incoming rocket. This time it landed behind him.

For the time being Raab realized he wasn't going anywhere. He looked back and saw what was left of the soldier who had just warned him. He and his protective log were gone. Raab checked his own body and was amazed he didn't have a scratch on him.

The rocket fire continued unabated for what seemed like a long time. Someone started calling in mortars that somewhat suppressed the rocket fire.

He decided it was time to move; undergrowth and a body were nothing to hide behind. Then he saw some movement on his right flank. A lone soldier was attacking a NVA bunker. He could see the man attempt to throw a hand grenade before he was cut down by fire from the bunker. The grenade blew up beside the fallen soldier. Raab knew the man was dead and that trying to get to him would be suicide. He was getting ready to try and move up the hill when a sergeant he didn't know dropped down beside him.

"We have orders to pull back. Get your ass back down the hill."

Raab was stunned. "We're almost at the top and now we fall back?" he thought.

The sergeant moved out to tell the soldiers Raab had been trying to get to. Raab crawled down to where there was some protection in the tree line. He found plenty of wounded men there and he went to work, doing what he could for them. He had patched up several of the men when he was ordered back further down the hill to help other medics who were trying to get the seriously wounded evacuated by the few choppers trying to make it into a very hot LZ.

The night was cold in the Central Highlands as Raab helped dig out an already started foxhole.

He slept little as he listened to the crying and moans of very scared men. He wondered how Tyler was doing. Raab suspected that in addition to his wounds, his arm was broken. He hadn't even mentioned it to Tyler when he had redressed his wound. It wouldn't send him home, but at least he would be out of this shit for awhile. He silently prayed for himself and the men around him.

He must have dozed off, because the next thing he heard was "Incoming!!" He pulled himself further down in the foxhole as mortars began to fall all around him as the sun was rising.

It was after noon before Raab could get out of his foxhole. He hadn't shit for a couple days and he needed to now. He crouched behind one of the standing trees and prayed he wouldn't be shot with his pants down. It was amazing how good the simple act of moving your bowels could feel, Raab thought.

While he had been ducking mortars all morning, the engineers from the rifle companies had managed to expand the LZ so that more than one helicopter could land at a time. The wounded from the night before and casualties from the morning mortar attack were loaded on the helicopters and evacuated.

When the wounded were gone, the grim task of loading the dead and flying them out began. Body bags were flown in by the 4th Division, which Raab learned had now joined the fight with the 173rd.

In the relative quiet of the afternoon, Raab hooked up once again with what was left of his platoon. He was surprised to find that Captain Powers, his company commander, was still alive. He looked just as surprised to see Raab.

"Jesus, Doc, we thought you got it yesterday when Lieutenant Thorton went down," he said. "Nobody saw you after that."

"It's been kind of confusing, sir," Raab answered, glad that he wasn't the only one left standing.

"I know, Doc. Listen we have a battalion surgeon at the LZ now. He has brought in medical supplies. I want you to resupply what you need. We're going back up that hill tomorrow.

Raab looked up again at Hill 875. It was starting to remind him of the battles he had read about and the movies about Pork Chop Hill, Iwo Jima and the Ranger assault up Point du Hoc on D-Day. Those guys had to go up a hundred foot vertical cliff as the Germans shot down at them. Well, he thought ,this fight will rank right up there with them, in the wasting of good infantry. The amazing thing was that like their predecessors, the Sky Soldiers wanted to take this hill. It meant something. It was a tangible piece of real estate they had paid for and now they were going to claim ownership.

At about 0900 Raab watched as F-IOO delivered tons of high explosives, napalm and cannon fire on the top of the hill. This time the planes were right on target. He saw this as a good sign.

With mortar fire leading the way, two companies of the 4th/503rd started back up the hill. The men ran firing and screaming at the bunkers in front of them. The NVA were returning mortar fire, and Raab watched in horror as several soldiers flew into the air and fell in a heap. He ran to them and found Sergeant Bechum, who was still alive, trying to get up and go up the out of his hill. Bechum had been one of his favorites since he joined the company. Raab pulled him down.

"Hey, Sarge, let me get a little of this bleeding stopped before you get going again," Raab told him, examining numerous shrapnel wounds to his back and legs. One had nicked his femoral artery and Raab went to work trying to stop it. He dug a hemostat out of his medical bag and, after several tries, was able to clamp the artery. He tapped down the clamp and covered the wound with a dressing. The other wounds could wait, right now he needed to get Bechum to the battalion aid station or he would die. He hadn't noticed, but SP/4 Wright, one of the other medics, had joined him and was giving aid to the other wounded. Over the din of the battle, he yelled out to Raab.

"John, two of these guys are dead. I can take care of the other two. Get the Sarge down the hill."

Raab nodded in agreement and, after giving Bechum a shot of morphine, began the arduous task of pulling him down the hill. Bechum, now in shock, was yelling that he wanted to go to the top with his men. Halfway down, Raab was met by additional medics. After giving them instructions about the hemostat, he started back up the hill. He could no longer remember how many times he had made that climb.

He could see the top now. There were Americans up there now; they fanned out across the summit. He had to be up there with them. He had earned it. By the time he reached the top, it was apparent the enemy had left. Paratroopers were clearing a landing zone they had blasted on top of the hill.

Raab finally did see a colonel on Hill 875. He came in to tell everyone to prepare for a counterattack. It never occurred and eventually the base had a turkey dinner flown out for the troops. Raab had totally forgotten it was Thanksgiving. He sat on the hill getting ready to eat his meal when a landing Huey threw up a massive amount of dirt and debris covering him and his meal. Raab looked down at the mess that was left. It just doesn't matter he told himself .... and ate his turkey dinner. It was anything but festive.

CHAPTER 22

Tyler looked out on the South China Sea. The sun was setting and the scene was peaceful. He had been flown by helicopter from Pleku to the 82nd Evacuation Hospital, in the not so beautiful coastal city of Qui Nhon, with a broken arm and several nasty shrapnel wounds.

He looked around at the other men in the hospital and realized he had been pretty lucky. The most serious of the wounded weren't here. They were in hospitals in Japan or on their way back to the States. He had learned that his unit, the 2nd/503rd had 87 men killed and 130 wounded on that fucking hill. Raab's unit had lost 28 and 123 wounded.

Jesus, he thought, maybe if they put the two together there might have enough men for a full company.

He was on painkillers, but his arm still hurt like hell. He had checked with several of the wounded from Raab's outfit, but either they didn't know his friend or didn't know if he made it or not. The Stars & Stripes newspaper had bold headlines about the big win on Hill 875 and theThanksgiving dinner. They made it sound like a backyard barbeque.

He was fortunate to have broken his left arm, as he was still able to write letters. The first one went to his parents. Tyler didn't want them to worry. He told them about his injuries and emphasized they would keep him out of the field for a while.

It was hard for him to believe he had only been in country for a couple months. It felt like he had spent his life here. He had written two letters to Patty, but had ripped them both up. Most nights he lay in the hospital bed thinking of her. It wasn't doing him any favors, he told himself. It just made him more depressed.

The following day, Tyler decided to write his old friend Tim Rowe. He probably had just played his last football game of the season with rival Harvard. It was unlikely that Yale would be in any post season bowls, but one never knew. Tyler found himself grinning for the first time since the battle. Yale in a bowl game, yeah right. Jesus, he missed playing! Maybe he would again. The doctors here told him his arm would be good as new ... just a big scar for the memory.

Dear Tim,

Since you go to Yale and read newspapers, I guess you might be up on the news from over here. I was in the first force that tried to get up Hill 875. You might have read we weren't too successful at first. I was wounded (not too bad) and I am in a hospital in Qui Nhon. It's on the coast of the South China Sea, but the waves suck. (Like I could find a surfboard in this God forsaken place). Anyway I literally ran into Raab on the battlefield. He put me on the helicopter that got me out of there. The bad news is as of this writing I don't know what happened to him.

I was real lucky, Tim. Somebody was watching over me. I actually prayed with John before I was medevaced. Anyway, being here, I think a lot about the things I took for granted back in the world.

Your friendship is one of those things. I want you to know I love you like a brother, the one neither of us had. In high school your influence kept me, well most of the time, on the right track. I've seen so much over here that it's hard to believe anyone will ever see home again, so I just wanted you to know that, just in case.

Well before I get totally mushy and depressed, I have some good news. One of the hospital medics told me the Army just opened up Australia as an R&R (rest & relaxation) site. I won't be eligible to go for a couple more months, but that's where I'll apply to go. It will be their summer there and I hear the surfing is great. Need to research this more while I am in this hospital.

So write back when you can. Tell me about the season and all the women you're sleeping around with.

Your bud,
Tyler

Tyler was finishing up letters to Petrov and Raab when he got some unexpected good news. A 4th /503rd paratrooper had been airlifted to the hospital from Dak To. This guy wasn't wounded however; he had malaria. Tyler sought him out to check up on Raab.

"I know Doc Raab," the paratrooper said during a lucid moment. "They have a song about him now, something about "Raab, Raab, you filthy skagg." You get the idea. I forget the rest of the words. You know he's kind of a legend, all the trips up Hill 875 and he didn't get a scratch; fucking unreal! Word is he's up for the Silver Star, among other shit. He's back at Dak To where they're trying to reorganize what is left of us."

"So why do they call him a filthy skagg?" Tyler asked, knowing how Raab was when it came to hygiene.

"Well … ever since the hill, he feels changing jungle fatigues is a waste of time. I am told he only brushes his teeth these days. Oh, I have something for you … if you're Taylor."

The paratrooper handed Tyler a thick letter. He thanked the soldier and went back to his bed, but changed his mind and decided to read it on the beach.

Tyler sat on the sand, his backed propped up against a piling for the pier. He pulled out the bulky letter and began to read.

Dear Tyler,

I am so relieved and happy to know you are recovering. I thought the worst of the fight had been seen by you. I was wrong. I hope one day we can sit around and talk about all that has happened to us and find something to laugh about. Right now that would be impossible for me. For now we're regrouping and I spend most of my days in the aid station here at Dak To. Any idea where you'll go after your release from the hospital? I hope we can be together; of course here isn't a great option!!!

I did have one sort of funny thing happen here. A major from division flew out here to see me. He was one of those spit-shined assholes who doesn't have a clue what happens out here in the real world. When he landed, even his helicopter was clean. As fate would have it, I am the first guy he runs into after getting off the bird. I was walking to the other side of the LZ to check on one of my walking wounded and encounter this base camp commando. The exchange went something like this.

"Soldier, you just failed to salute me," the red faced major blurts out as we pass.

"Sir, that's because you're in the field; you know, a combat zone and we don't salute out here," I answer with sincere respect. The major looks me over from head to stem.

"Soldier, you're a disgrace. Look at you, your uniform is torn and filthy, your boots aren't polished and when was the last time you stood close to a razor?"

His face is really getting red now, Tyler. I should have shut up, but he pissed me off so I answered.

"You know, sir, what you need to do is get your sorry ass out here with the troops and out of your air conditioned office. We'll see how you look after a month or so humping in the jungle."

I walked away with his jaw hanging around the top of the spit shined boots.

The rest of the story was told to me by Sergeant Wilcox, he's Captain Powers' top aide. (Powers is my CO. He was on the Hill) Anyway, this major burst into the command post, mad as hell, and finds Powers. He pulls him outside and points to me.

"Captain, I want that insubordinate son-of-a bitch put on report, demoted and whatever else you can think of," he says. "I've never seen anyone like him before under my command."

The major had to sit down then and get a drink of water. I guess he was exhausted, Tyler. So when he finally recovers, Wilcox says he asks the captain the following:

"Now that I know you will take care of that disgraceful soldier, let's get on to why I am out here. Specialist/5 John Raab has been awarded the Silver Star for his actions on Hill 785. I understand he is one of your finest medics, captain. It would be a pleasure to meet him and let him know about the awards ceremony. You know, General Williams will be there personally."

Wilcox is cracking up now, along with Powers, who's trying to be respectful. The major is looking at them like they lost it.

"I am sorry sir," Powers says, "But you just met Sp/5 Raab."

The major just looks at them and walks back to his helicopter, saying nothing. Wilcox tells me it's the first good laugh he's had in a month.

Oh, by the way, I am now SP/5 Raab; got promoted right after getting back here to Dak To. Reason given: Everyone else is dead.

Ah the Army Tyler, don't you love it? Captain Powers talked to me later about my transgressions. I promised I would be nicer in the future. I don't think he believes me, but after all, in the Army's eyes I am now a war HERO.

The other rumor I heard was you were up for a bunch of things. We better write Petrov and tell him to get on the ball!!!

I included the Stars & Stripes issue that talks about the 173rd and our heroic efforts to eat Thanksgiving dinner on a hill with a view. I hope to be seeing you soon. Tough guy that you are ... I still pray for you John Tyler reread the letter, laughed out loud, then tore open the letter to Tim and updated that Raab was fine.

CHAPTER 23

"Come on baby light my fire. Come on baby light my fire. Try to set the night on fire."

Mike Petrov sang the Doors popular lyrics which he knew was a song about smoking pot. Too bad Jim Morrison was never in Vietnam. If he was up here in this Huey helicopter watching the crazy colors of this explosive display put on by competing artillery, mortars and Puff the Magic Dragon, the nickname of the C-47 aircraft that was firing 5,400 rounds a minute, well he would have thought pot was pretty tame. The night really was on fire here.

Such were Petrov's thoughts as he monitored the prone soldier on the stretcher next to him. Private "Numbnuts" had accidentally shot himself in the chest while setting up for the night in the jungle. Petrov had bandaged the wound. The bullet had luckily exited through the top of the shoulder and spared the "cherries," vital parts.

The patrol's captain thought Petrov should accompany the soldier back to the hospital in Cu Chi, which It was fine with Petrov. He would be sleeping in a bed instead of a foxhole. While in the helicopter he got an IV inserted and running. The morphine had kicked in and his patient was relaxed.

Petrov sat back against the fuselage and thought about his buddies who had been working on real combat wounds. He received letters from both, Tyler from the hospital in Qui Nhon and Raab from Dak To. Before he heard from them, he figured they were both dead. He had heard repeated rumors at Cu Chi that all the airborne medics had been killed on Hill 875. He had been in total depression until he received their letters. Privately, he was glad he was assigned to the 25th Infantry. His unit had not been involved in any sustained combat. Hit and miss encounters with the Viet Cong was the most excitement he had seen. His biggest gripe was the constant patrols, night ambushes and -- worst thing of all -- digging those damn foxholes every time they moved.

He doubted he would be making E-5 like Tyler and Raab. There were plenty of medics in his company and most of them were lifers. He figured they would get any promotions that might come up. It gave him something to bitch about at the least.

He spun around and sat at the edge of the helicopters open door. In the distance he could see the lights of Saigon. It was the only thing illuminated in this strange land. Christmas was a week away and you would never know it here ; just another day in the bush for a grunt. He remembered Tyler had told him he had volunteered for the Infantry in basic, and the sergeant told him that the Infantry was for the dumb guys who couldn't be trained for anything else. Petrov had learned that certainly wasn't the case. Sure there were knuckleheads like the guy who shot himself tonight. They were the exception as far as he was concerned. The majority were smart and tough. They could take it and he was proud to be their medic. The door gunner interrupted his thoughts.

"Hey, Doc, we're going in."

The gunner pointed down at the airfield Petrov could see in the distance. He checked his patient one last time and found he was either asleep or unconscious. Either way was fine with him.

Medics from the hospital met them as they touched down. Petrov briefed one of them about what had happened and the treatment he had given. He walked with them to the hospital and watched them take the soldier directly into the OR.

It was still early and he decided to get a beer at the enlisted men's club.

The club was dark inside. Petrov mused that it was such a dump, they had to keep it dark. He ordered a pitcher of beer and sat at the bar by himself. Most of the troops here were REMFs -- rear-echelon motherfuckers. The guys from the field usually didn't associate with them and the REMF's avoided the combat troops.

They had entertainment though, a Filipino band with a good looking lead singer. Her songs were in English, sung with a heavy accent. He started to relax and enjoy the music when he felt a heavy hand on his shoulder.

"Hey, Mike what are you doing in here? Thought you were out in the boonies."

Petrov turned to see the grinning face of Sergeant Welsh, the senior medic for the battalion and his immediate boss. Welsh was a very large, no-nonsense black man from the South. While Petrov was somewhat intimidated by his size, he sensed Welsh liked him.

"I came in on a dust-off, Sarge. One of the FNG's shot himself when we were digging in for the night. The captain sent me in with him to hold his hand, I guess."

Welsh nodded.

"Fucking new guys are always doing something dumb out there," Welsh said. "Hell, at least you can sleep on a cot tonight."

Welsh sat down next to Petrov and ordered bourbon. It drove Petrov crazy that he couldn't order a hard drink, not because of his age, because of his rank. You had to be an E-5 to purchase hard liquor.

"So, Mike what are you going to do after this little stint in the Army?" Welsh asked sipping his drink.

" Going back to college. I completed a couple years at a JC in California. I think I want to be an engineer."

"That's good, Mike. I never had the chance to go to school. I was probably lucky they let me in the Army. All the education I ever got was in this man's Army."

Welsh looked up at the ceiling and they drank in silence for awhile.

Petrov started to say something when a fight started up near the band. Welsh jumped up immediately and Petrov followed him up to the combatants. It was two white guys pounding on each other. The big sergeant separated them.

"You assholes take this outside."

The two soldiers took one look at the massive sergeant and moved towards the door. "You watch tomorrow, Mike, one of those REMFs will be in asking us to patch him up. That's all I do here is take care of a bunch of wieners. I wish I could go out in the field once in a while. I just too damn old."

They drank for another couple hours, then stumbled back to the barracks. It was one of the few nights Petrov slept well. By noon the next day he was on a Huey heading back out to his company -- and more

CHAPTER 24

Tyler woke up to a scream and realized he was the one screaming. He was sweating, but knew immediately he wasn't on the Hill. He was in a hospital bed. Lieutenant McDonald, the cute young night nurse, came over and held his hand.

"You're OK now, Taylor," she said. "You had a nightmare."

Tyler was now fully awake and a little embarrassed.

"I am fine, lieutenant. Thank you."

She smiled down at him.

"Try to sleep, Taylor," she said. "You'll be out of here before you know it."

Tyler watched her as she walked off. If he had been back in college, he would have made a play for her. Not now in the two class world that was the Army. She was an officer and he was an enlisted man. At least he was now a Specialist/5. Two days before, the battalion colonel walked in and pinned a Purple Heart, a Bronze Star with a V and a Combat Medical Badge on Tyler's chest, then advised him he had been promoted.

Tyler's arm had almost healed and he expected it would only be a matter of days before he would be discharged from the hospital. He had already been told he would be returned to Dak To.

On Christmas morning, he began looking for Raab at the Dak To compound. He didn't have to look very hard to find his friend. Actually he heard him before he saw him. He was telling a bunch of newly arrived "cherry" medics how they might survive in the jungle. It was classic Raab. He had the men hanging on his every word. Tyler listened outside the tented aid station until Raab finished his speech.

"If you listen to that son-of-a bitch, for sure you won't make it," Tyler yelled from outside the tent.

Raab jumped up as Tyler stepped inside.

"Merry Christmas, John!" The two men embraced each other.

"Jesus ,Tyler, it's so good to see you! How's the arm?"

"I'm good, John."

Raab looked over at one of the new medics. "Hey, get this man a cold beer."

The young soldier jumped up and went outside to a cooler to get a beer for the new arrival. Tyler sat down across from his friend on one of the personal trunks that lined the tent. The medic returned with a beer and handed it to Tyler. It was cold.

"Where in the world did you get ice, John?" Tyler asked as he enjoyed the rare treat of a cold beer.

"They have to provide it so we can keep our vaccines chilled," Raab said with a smile. "We always manage to get a little extra for beer and of course my cokes."

"You guys, this is Tyler Taylor. He's the medic I have told you about." The other medics all nodded and one saluted Tyler.

"They all know what you did on the Hill, Tyler."

Tyler, somewhat embarrassed, just sipped on his beer. He changed the subject quickly. "I hear the 173rd going to be split up, John. They're sending me to some place called Ban Me Thuot with what's left of the 2nd/503rd."

"I know," Raab replied. "I am going to Tuy Hoa. Pretty soon, I guess. We were hit hard, Tyler."

Tyler lowered his head and nodded in the affirmative. Raab could see his friend was hurting.

"Hey, Tyler, I guess the cooks are going to actually try and serve a Christmas dinner tonight. I know you're not big on church, but maybe you'll consider going to Mass with me this afternoon."

"I think I'd like that, John."

They spent the rest of the morning talking about all the things they were going to do once they got back home. The first sergeant stopped by to wish everyone a Merry Christmas. He was surprised to see Tyler.

"We have some mail we've been saving for you, Taylor," he said. "It's at the command post. Glad you're back."

After he left, Tyler and Raab walked over to the CP to pick up the mail. Tyler quickly looked through it. He saw that most of the letters were from his parents before he was wounded. One of the letters was post marked Washington, D.C. He opened it as soon as he got back to the aid tent. It was from Private Howland, the soldier with the serious leg wound Tyler had treated on the Hill. He silently read the letter.

Dear SP/4 Taylor,

I hope you remember me because you saved my life on Hill 875. I was the guy with the bullet hole in his leg among other things. I will always remember your kindness to me. You probably didn't even know my name, but it's Brian Howland. I don't even know if you survived, but I still needed to send this letter and hope it gets to you and you're well.

The doctors told me if it wasn't for your care, I wouldn't be alive. I am sorry to say that they weren't able to save my leg. It was amputated after I was flown to Japan. I am now at Walter Reed Hospital in D.C. It's close to my family home in Maryland and my folks can visit almost every weekend. The doctors tell me they have come a long way with prosthetic legs and after I get stronger, I will go into a rehab program.

Do you know I don't even know your first name, Taylor, yet you

*risked your life to save mine. I want you to know that I am glad to
be alive. I am going to be back with my family and friends soon. I
hope someday to thank you in person.*

   Please write if you can.

Brian Howland

Tyler finished the letter and handed it to Raab. As he read it, a tear
rolled down his cheek.

"This one's a keeper, Tyler. Let's go say a prayer of thanks."

He handed the letter back to Tyler. The two friends walked over to
a tent with a makeshift altar. During Mass, Tyler felt relief for the first
time since the battle. He prayed for God to guide him. With Raab's
urging he took communion and was at peace. He was glad he was a
medic and had saved a life. He thought of his family and his friends.
These were the things that counted, he thought. Why had he been angry
for so long? He had been given so much and he wasted it. Not anymore,
he thought. If he survived this war, things would be different.

Before Tyler and Raab departed Dak To for their new assignments,
a memorial service was held for the Sky Soldiers killed on Hill 875. It
was called a "boots" ceremony.

Rows of jump boots were placed in line, each pair representing
a soldier. The chaplains all offered prayers. Posthumous medals were
awarded, as well as ones for the soldiers who had survived. SP/5 John
Raab was awarded the Silver Star, the third highest award for combat
valor.

Tyler's heart pounded as he watched his humble friend stand at
attention as the medal was pinned on by General Williams. There was
no jubilation even when the general announced that in recognition
for their outstanding valor during battles around Dak To, the 173rd
Airborne Brigade was awarded the Presidential Unit Citation.

It was a sad occasion, remembering all who had been wounded or
died.

CHAPTER 25

The 173rd Airborne was split up after that. Tyler reported for duty at Ban Me Thuot and Raab remained near Tuy Hoa. After arriving, Tyler was happy to see the fire base was ringed with tanks from the 69th Armor. It was common knowledge that the VC did not like messing with the tanks and he felt a little safer with their presence. He was assigned to the Civil Affairs Team as their medic.

Ban Me Thuot was in Dac Lac Province, near the Cambodian border. It was 180 km from Pleiku. One of the first things Tyler learned about the place was that Teddy Roosevelt had hunted tigers there. Supposedly one of his old hunting lodges was still intact somewhere out in the jungle.

The first couple of weeks there were spent with the team learning about the Montagnards and their traditions. Tyler's new lieutenant explained that the Montagnards liked us and the Army wanted it to stay that way. Special Forces in the area recruited the young men for the Mobile Strike Force Command or MIKE Force. Tyler's team provided support for the villages and tried to gain their trust and gather good intelligence about the VC in the area. There were several civilian agencies that also helped the indigenous tribes. The Agency for International

Development supported a leprosarium and Tyler was told the team occasionally helped out with the medical care of the lepers.

The term Montagnard means "mountain people" Tyler learned. It was French, from the French colonial period in Vietnam. There were several tribes in the Central Highlands with overlapping customs and language patterns. Among them were the Jarai, Koho, Manong and Rhade.

"I was told they were originally some type of Polynesians," Sergeant Capatosto explained to Tyler. He seemed to know a lot about them and Tyler listened attentively.

"We'll work mostly with the Jarai," Capatosto said. "The Vietnamese don't like them. They call them moi, which means savage. Can you believe that, Tyler? Who the fuck is more savage than the VC and NVA?"

Tyler just nodded and listened to the sergeant recount some of his many encounters with the "Yards," as he called the Montagnards.

"One thing you never want to do is pay much attention to their women. They are topless and after all this time in the boonies you tend to look," he said. "Also, Doc, be careful where you touch if you have to examine them. The men are very good with their machetes, if you get what I mean. It's one of the many reasons the regular grunts are not allowed in the villages. Oh, one last thing Taylor, they like to drink and smoke pot." Capatosto said with a wink and a smile.

He was pretty well versed by the time he entered one of the villages with the team.

"Is the kid going to make it, Doc?"

Tyler looked up at Lieutenant Phillips, his stethoscope still in his ears.

"He has pneumonia, lieutenant," Tyler said. "Both lungs are filling up."

The Montagnards believed that when someone was sick, the best thing they could do was to heat up their hut and cover the person with blankets. It reminded Tyler of the American Indian sweat lodges he had read about.

"The kid has a fever of 104 and his breathing is shallow," he said. "I am going to try penicillin and try to convince his mother she needs to cool him down."

Later, after giving the small boy a shot of penicillin and a piece of candy, he tried to explain to Edu, the team's interpreter, why it was best not to have a smoky fire in the hut. He wasn't sure if his advice was lost in translation, but the mother seemed to be listening as Edu conveyed the advice.

And so went Tyler's first day as a Civil Affairs medic. He was amazed at the long lines of patients who waited to see him at the aid station he and one of the other team members had set up at the rear of their Jeep.

By the late afternoon he had treated the most serious wounds. The little kids were waiting for anything he might give them. He handed each small hand what he had the most of -- band aids.

Sergeant Capatosto came over as Tyler was putting away the remainder of his supplies. Tyler was finding out the young Italian from New York was one of the most likeable guys on the team. He had really made an effort to make him feel welcome. He had learned that Capatosto already had a masters from NYU and spoke fluent Jarai Montagnard. He had been helping Tyler learn a few basic words over beers at the fire base.

"How'd you like your first day, Doc?" Capatosto said, kneeling down on one knee and looking towards the village. He'd seen some combat too, Tyler thought.

"It actually was great, Sarge," Tyler said. "It's the first time I felt like I had helped someone other than our soldiers. I guess you're pretty used to all this."

Capatosto ignored the question. "I hear you saw a lot of action at Dak To, Tyler?"

Tyler only nodded at first. "I haven't talked about it for a while, Sarge. Let's just say the scenery is a lot better here."

"I understand, Doc. Helping people is a much better gig. By the way, Doc, my first name is Sal. I prefer that. I am not all that military. I was drafted. The L.T. is pretty cool too. Went into ROTC just to get through college."

Tyler smiled. "Well at least you guys finished college. I sorta got kicked out. It's a long story I'll have to tell you over a bottle of Jack Daniels."

"I'll look forward to the Jack Daniels and the story," Capatosto said. "Right now the chief is setting up some liquid refreshment of his own. Ever drink rice wine, Doc?"

For the next several hours, Tyler learned all about the ritual of drinking wine with the Montagnards. You drank in the order of your importance as determined by the chief. The same was true for the order in which the wines were drunk. The best wine was consumed first and so on down the line. The wine was made and stored in large ceramic vases. Sal told Tyler he didn't want to know about the fermenting process. All he said was that it "was gross." The top of the vase was stuffed with banana leafs and a little wooden bamboo strip with a descending notched strip on top of the opening. Bamboo straws were inserted into the vase to drink from.

Tyler found out about the bamboo strip and its purpose after sitting down in front of the first vase. The Montagnards didn't like drinking "cheaters." They would pour in water over the leaves. The water level would come up to the top of the notched strip. The "honest" drinker had to drink until the notch was no longer covered with water. No pretending you took a drink.

By the fourth vase, Tyler was feeling blissfully loose. While there were three more vases laid out, the lieutenant called time. The sun was going down and Vietnam would soon become Charlies' land again.

SP/5 Taylor needed to sober up and be a soldier again. They were back at the fire base 45 minutes later. After a box of C-rations, Tyler crashed on his cot and wondered what tomorrow would bring to this land of contradictions.

CHAPTER 26

The breadfruit tree was probably 50 feet high. Raab lay under it and inhaled the sweet orange fragrance. All of a sudden it was like he was somewhere else. He closed his eyes and imagined he was back home. He wasn't, of course. The Central Highlands jungle was all around him. He took in the little pleasure. It was a lot better than smelling sweaty, dirty soldiers who had been moving through the jungle for the past two days. That included himself. His reverie was interrupted by Lieutenant Dryer, who laid down next to him.

"Hey, Doc, how's it hanging?" Dryer said, not waiting for an answer.

"We're here until the sun goes down , then we need to hump at least a couple more clicks up the mountain just in case Charlie got a glimpse of us today," he said.

The lieutenant had never looked at Raab. Instead he kept his gaze down the hill into the valley below them. It was standard operating procedure for ambush patrols to move out after their initial setup, just in case.

Raab was the only medic on the 10 man patrol. He probably should have sent one of the new medics he was breaking in. He just figured they weren't ready yet. In the back of his mind he knew the real answer. He couldn't stand to have someone killed he had sent out. The captain had talked to him about it once already. At least he hadn't told Raab he couldn't go out. So here he was on yet another patrol.

The men lay silently, waiting for the sun to set and they would then move further up the mountain. Raab had learned from other nights in the jungle that fruit bats loved breadfruit trees. They would be zooming in any time. Raab did not like bats, rats or snakes. He looked up to make sure none had arrived just yet. They hadn't, but he was restless to move out. Why was it, he asked himself, that there was always something bad to counter the good in a thing? The smell of the tree was wonderful, but the bats would soon ruin it for him.

Two hours later, when the patrol had settled in for the long night, Raab finally nodded off for a short nap. He was to have the 2-4 a.m. guard duty. Their new position was even higher than the previous one. It had been a struggle moving up the hill in the darkness and Raab was exhausted.

His dreams took him back to Chris Rowe. She was there a lot of the time now, even as he reminded himself it could never work out for them. Even so, he found himself back in the pool with her, admiring her beauty and brains. She was touching his shoulder, shaking him.

"Doc, it's your watch." Raab woke to see Corporal Samuels kneeling beside him.

Raab sat up to let Samuels know he was awake. Samuels crawled off to get his own troubled sleep. Looking out into the darkness, Raab peered down into the valley.

For a change it wasn't raining and a full moon lit up the jungle terrain. He listened intently for any change in the normal sounds and was happy he detected none. He looked at his watch and saw it was a little after 2 in the morning.

In these quiet times, even surrounded by the other men, he felt alone. It was then he would think about the dead and wounded men he had seen. The horrors of the Hill. He would always call on God to help him. He didn't want to have all the problems he had read about that returning soldiers were experiencing; post traumatic stress was what the shrinks called it. Young men unable to cope with what they had seen. He hoped his faith would pull him through it -- if of course, he survived the rest of this year. He tried not to think about that, but the odds were against him. He was, after all, a combat medic, and their survival rate wasn't good.

About an hour later, Raab saw what he thought was a man run down the path far below him. For a minute Raab thought his mind was playing tricks on him. That would happen at night when you were on guard. You would stare so intently out into the jungle that ; you finally imagined someone or something. But a short time later the man reappeared and ran back in the direction he had come from. Raab immediately started waking the men on either side him and in a minute the lieutenant crawled over to be briefed on what he had seen.

"I think he was a scout, Lieutenant, and he probably has friends."

Lieutenant Dryer took out his binoculars and scanned the area below. A couple minutes later, a VC patrol emerged from the jungle and passed in single file about 200 yards below them. The force was much larger than Raab had expected. He counted at least 50 men moving across the valley floor. Dryer made what Raab thought was a great decision. He did nothing.

Their 10-man patrol was not equipped to take on that many enemy. It would be suicide. They lay in silence and watched the rear guard of the VC patrol look back in their direction, then melt into the darkness of the jungle.

Neither Raab nor the other men slept after that sighting. Dryer kept them on the ground for several hours after the sun came up, making sure the VC didn't return. After being reasonably sure that they wouldn't walk headlong into an ambush, they started down into the valley. It was five long hours later that Dryer felt safe enough to call in helicopters for extraction.

At the base camp, the men sat down for their first hot meal in five days. Raab was starting on his second serving of what appeared to be beef stew when Lieutenant Dryer entered the mess hall and sat with the rest of his patrol.

"I let Intel know about our sighting. They're going to work over the area tonight with artillery and "Puff the Magic Dragon." CO didn't even question why we didn't engage. No more fucking suicide missions for him after the Hill I would guess. You guys can get some sleep for now. He didn't give me any further orders for now."

The lieutenant got up and left the mess after having a cup of coffee.

"What do you think Doc, he's pretty squared away right?"

Private Wade anxiously looked at Raab. He was one of the new members of the patrol and he had yet to experience combat.

Raab gave him one of his trademark stares and pulled the young private to within a couple inches of his face.

"Well, Wade, you're not dead yet, so I guess so."

The young soldier's eyes widened as he watched Raab get up and leave the mess tent.

"Jesus, he really is crazy like everyone says," Wade said to the other amused soldiers at the table as he walked out.

Sergeant Ambrose, the platoon leader, looked up from his half eaten meal, not smiling.

"I'll tell you something, boy. He is crazy, but if your shit is hanging out there someday, there is no one else you would rather have with you. You remember that and you might just live to repeat this story someday."

CHAPTER 27

The first day of the new year, that's what Tet was. This was a time in the Vietnamese culture when families paint their homes, get new clothes, pay their debts. They are supposed to be very careful about what they do so good fortune is assured for the year. Gifts are exchanged and the people pray for prosperity and good health. Fireworks like the 4th of July. Anyway that's what Petrov had been told.

The VC and NVA had called for a truce during the holiday. He was back at Cu Chi and was getting a well deserved rest from the field. He was laying on his bunk at the medical headquarters when Sergeant Welsh walked up to him.

"Hey, Mike, don't you have some buddies in the Central Highlands with the 173rd?"

Petrov sat up on his bunk and waited for the next words from his sergeant.

"Well they just got hit hard last night at Dak To and Ban Me Thuot," Welsh said. "I just came from HQ and they want us to be ready. You better get your gear together. Evidently Charlie doesn't believe in holidays. I'll find out where we're going."

Petrov was putting together his aid bag and checking his .45 and AR-15 when Welsh returned. Back to the jungle, Petrov thought.

"Mike, you're going with the ready reaction team to Tan Son Nhut airbase," Welsh said. "The damn VC have almost overrun it. Evidently some ARVN paratroopers are holding it for now."

The view from their helicopter was scary. Petrov looked out at the smoke from dozens of fires. Gunshots could be heard from below them. People ran in all directions to escape. Saigon was one big battlefield.

Their helicopter came under fire as they tried to land near one of the hangars. The pilot banked hard and pulled up towards the northwest end of the airport. He was able to land there and Petrov found himself running with the other soldiers back in the direction they had just come from. Up to this point he had been secretly happy that he hadn't joined Raab and Taylor with the 173rd. All the combat they had seen and he was hardly in anything that dangerous. Now he was the one in deep shit. Not in the jungle, but on concrete.

There was a heavy concentration of rocket and mortar fire in front of them. The noise was deafening and it was hard to hear the orders being given by the young lieutenant leading them. Petrov didn't even know his name. The group took cover behind what Petrov thought was maybe an office building. He peeked out around the corner of the building and saw about 30 VC running across the tarmac towards an open hangar. He opened up with the AR-15 and watched as one of the soldiers in his sights went down. A small smile came to his face. Finally, he thought, I got to shoot one of them.

The lieutenant came up with the radioman.

"Doc, the guys from the other chopper report they have two guys down and one walking wounded. They're over behind that hangar. They don't have a medic. I'll send Garcia and Jones with you for cover. Their RDO can call in your medevac."

The lieutenant pointed to a hangar just to the north. Petrov and the other two men made a sprint towards it. The first man Petrov checked on was already dead. He worked on the second while the fight continued just in front of them. Most of the men were lying on the ground directing a steady stream of fire at the now entrenched VC. Petrov successfully stopped the heavy bleeding from a head wound, most likely the result of shrapnel. There was so much blood it was hard to tell. The man had numerous other wounds that were not life threatening, and Petrov moved on to another wounded soldier. He too had been hit by either mortar or rocket fire. His right arm was almost completely severed and the man screamed out as he lay on the ground staring at it. Petrov was able to get a tourniquet on above what he was sure would later be an amputated arm. The man calmed somewhat after Petrov shot him with two shots of morphine. He wrapped what was left of the arm tight into the soldiers body then turned to the RDO.

"We need a medevac now." The RDO shook his head in the affirmative and spoke into his microphone.

Petrov yelled at Garcia. "We need a couple stretchers for these guys when the dust-off lands," he said.

"OK, Doc, we'll get 'em," Garcia shouted back before scuttling off.

Petrov had returned to his first patient to find him unconscious but breathing. That helicopter better get it in gear, he thought, if these guys are going to make it.

A short time later the familiar thump-thump of the rotor could be heard in the distance. The helicopter landed about 25 yards from their position. Garcia and another soldier ran out and retrieved the needed stretchers for the wounded men. After getting more help from the still embattled platoon, the men were carried to the medevac and lifted off safely.

"We need to move up to the hangar, Doc," the platoon sergeant yelled at Petrov as he gathered his medical bag from the ground.

Petrov looked around and only the seven soldiers who had helped load the wounded were still with him. He looked towards the hangar and could see the remainder of the platoon taking up defensive positions on the south end.

He started running with the men to the hangar. He had only gone about 20 yards when he felt himself being lifted into the air and then falling violently to earth. At first all he heard was a ringing in his ears. He looked over to see a soldier on the ground, his face blackened, most of his leg blown away. He was saying something to him, but Petrov couldn't understand because of the damn ringing sound. Gradually the ringing lessened and he could hear the soldier crying out to him for help. Petrov tried to get up and realized he couldn't. He looked down to see he was covered in blood. It was odd, he thought, he wasn't in pain, just having trouble breathing. He lay back and closed his eyes. He was ready to die.

It was a wonderful dream. He was back in high school and was sailing on his friend's father's 45-foot sailboat. It was spring break and he had been invited along for a overnight sail to Catalina Island. He was riding on the bow and felt the gentle lapping of the waves as the boat cleanly cut through them. He could see the island in front of him as the boat turned towards Avalon. Someone was calling him now breaking this pleasant moment.

"Petrov. Petrov wake up, son. Come on now. Wake up."

Petrov tried to open his eyes. It was hard to focus. Where was he?

"Petrov, I am Dr. Gable. You are on a Navy hospital ship. You were wounded at the airport. Can you remember?"

Petrov nodded in the affirmative. His mouth was so dry. He managed to say "water."

The doctor said something to a someone across the room and soon a corpsman held a straw to Petrov's parched lips. He sucked in the water as the doctor continued to talk.

"Michael, you have a compound fracture to your left leg, and we repaired a perforation to your right lung. You have numerous shrapnel wounds, but the good news is you'll heal just fine. You were very lucky a Navy SEAL team coming into the airport saw the mortar explosion that caused your injuries. A corpsman on the team was able to treat you almost immediately. You had a sucking chest wound that could have killed you. He got you stabilized and brought you here on their helicopter. We have notified the Army. When you are healthy enough you'll be transferred back to them and I imagine your next stop will be the Army hospital in Japan and then back home. The war is over for you, son."

Petrov was trying very hard to take this all in. "Did anyone else make it, Doctor?" he asked.

A stern but sad look came across the surgeons face.

"I am sorry to say that just you and two other soldiers were brought here," Dr. Gable said. "I have no information on the men you were with when you were wounded. Try to get some sleep now."

Petrov closed his eyes. The drugs were doing their thing, he thought. Just as he was drifting off, he felt the rolling of the ship on the water. Maybe he could dream again about sailing.

CHAPTER 28

Tyler almost felt sorry for the enemy soldiers who attacked them. He watched from a bunker as the tanks from the 69th Armor fired beehive rounds from their big guns. The VC were almost cut in two from the non-stop fusillade. Within an hour the enemy had withdrawn and evidently decided the nearby ARVN troops would be a little easier to deal with. After the battle, he had walked out with one of the infantry platoons to get a body count. He was almost overwhelmed with the carnage. It was surreal.

While the fighting in the Central Highlands was intense, Tyler spent most of the next two weeks at the fire base pulling guard duty at night and manning the aid station during the day. He was not involved in any direct combat or assigned any missions. The intelligence reports suggested the Montagnards took a beating from the local VC and his team was anxious to check on the villages. They were finally allowed to leave the fire base the third week of February; what they found wasn't pretty.

Tyler had set up some portable tables and stretcher for the first med-cap. The village was a disaster area. The Montagnards silently lined up for treatment. This time it wasn't minor cuts and infections. Gunshot wounds were common among those who had survived the attack on the small village. Many of the young men had been kidnapped and had just disappeared into the surrounding jungle with their VC captors

The Vietnamese would not allow Montagnards into their hospitals. The care the villagers would receive could only come from the team. Captain Greenley, the battalion surgeon, was attempting to treat a middle aged woman who had a gunshot wound to her right thigh.

"Taylor, can you help me out here for a minute?"

Tyler had Sergeant Capatosto hold pressure on a compress he was applying to a machete slash that an elder tribesman had received to the top of his head. It would require stitches later to close it correctly. He walked over to help the surgeon.

"Look at this mess, Tyler."

Tyler looked down at an infected gunshot wound and knew immediately it would require surgery if the woman was to keep her leg. He helped turn the woman over so Greenley could look at the backside of the wound. There was no exit. The bullet was still in her leg.

"We can't help her here," he said. "We'll have to take her back with us. Round up Edu so he can explain to the chief she needs to go with us."

The young surgeon placed a compress on the wound and administered a shot of morphine. Tyler left to find the interpreter.

After several more hours of work, the team left with the woman. The chief had reluctantly granted permission for her to leave with the American soldiers. After arriving at the fire base, Tyler recruited a couple other medics for the surgery. A anesthesiologist had been flown in from the 71st Evac Hospital in Pleiku. It was a crude operating room, but the surgery went well. Captain Greenley was able to locate the bullet and remove it. Debridement of the wound was extensive. The necrotic tissue was removed and a large amount of penicillin was given to the patient. There was no way she would be able to return to her village for some time.

Tyler was exhausted after he finally was able to collapse on his cot in the medical tent. He was about to doze off when he noticed someone had left mail on his trunk. The letter on top was from Petrov. He knew something was wrong immediately when he noticed the postmark. It was supposed to be the APO used in Vietnam. This one was San Francisco which was used for overseas mail in the Pacific, other than Vietnam. Tyler tore open the envelope and found a one page letter inside.

Tyler,

The best thing I can say is that I am alive. I was hit during the Tet offensive in Saigon. I am at Camp Zama in Japan now; undergoing treatment. I have a collapsed lung, broken leg and a lot of shrapnel wounds. They tell me that after I heal a little, I'll be shipped to the States.

Lots of details I'll share later. I don't feel like writing much now. I wanted you and Raab to know what happened to me. I hope we can talk about all this someday over a beer. I will tell you one interesting thing ... I was rescued by the Navy. Go figure.

When I settle somewhere, I'll send an address. I hope you're safe. I heard the Central Highland's was pretty lit up during Tet.

Mike

Tyler finished the letter and immediately thought about Raab. He hadn't heard from him, either, but if anything happened he would have heard about it. He had conflicting thoughts about Mike. It was sad his friend had been severely wounded, but he would see home again. It didn't appear from his letter that any of his injuries would be permanent. He had seen so many men whose injuries would be a daily reminder ... for the rest of their lives. And a lot whose headstones would forever speak of their sacrifice.

All of a sudden tears began to flow down Tyler's face. He wondered if he could take all the stress and sadness much longer. He needed to get out of here, if even for just a little while. He was eligible for R&R, or rest and relaxation as the Army called it. He needed a lot of both. One of the recurring thoughts he had about R&R was that if he didn't survive this war, what was the last thing he would want to do. Of course on top of the list was seeing his parents and friends, like Tim Rowe. Well, that wasn't going to happen. The only R&R close to home was Hawaii. It was an unwritten rule to save those spots for the soldiers who were married. His second choice was easy -- surfing.

Australia had opened up recently as one of the options. He had read about the massive surf on their east coast. The problem was a lack of any information about getting around. Could you rent a board and where would you go? Most guys just went to Bangkok or some other Asian country with cheap booze and women. He had no desire for that. What he needed was water. It was always welcoming, almost spiritual. Anyway he would apply tomorrow. He closed his eyes and said a silent prayer for Mike. He fell asleep almost immediately.

CHAPTER 29

I t was a week before the Montagnard woman could travel. Edu talked to her daily and tried to keep her spirits up. She had been very apprehensive about her stay with the medics of the 173rd. Tyler had changed her dressings at least twice a day and the penicillin had worked to perfection. Captain Greenley closed the wound just prior to releasing her. It would leave a nasty scar, but she would be fine. She was able to sit in the front of the Jeep on their return to the village.

The village seemed empty as they neared the raised huts. A young boy ran up to Edu and looked almost scared when he saw the woman. He spoke excitedly to the interpreter, who smiled ever so slightly as he nodded in the affirmative.

"He says we have arrived in time for her funeral." Edu spoke softly to Lieutenant Phillips, motioning towards the woman.

"She is Lam, the wife of Kpuh. He is the one you call the chief of the village."

Tyler couldn't believe that she had spent the week at their compound and never mentioned she was the chief's wife. As word spread of her return the villagers came out to welcome her back. She was soon surrounded by several women, who lead her to her hut.

The chief spoke with Edu and motioned several times towards Tyler and the other men of the Civil Affairs Team.

"Instead of a funeral, we are now invited to a feast to celebrate Lam's return from the spirit world." Edu again spoke directly to the lieutenant.

"Tell Chief Kpuh that we would be honored to attend the celebration," he said.

Edu quickly translated the message to the Chief Kpuh, who smiled broadly.

The rest of the day was spent drinking rice wine and eating pork. One of the children brought an egg to Tyler. It was hard boiled and upon closer inspection, he could see the embryo had started to form before it was cooked. He politely declined.

The climax of the day came just as the team was preparing to leave. The chief presented a copper Montagnard bracelet to the lieutenant and Tyler. He bowed to them as he placed each bracelet on the soldiers wrist.

Capatosto explained the ceremony to Tyler and the lieutenant as the chief stood in front of them.

"Sir, you and Taylor are now members of the chief's family. It's important that you wear no other bracelet but his. The Army guys you see with half a dozen of them on their wrists don't understand the significance of this honor. They just buy them in Pleku. This bracelet, you will note, is marked with symbols of the chief's family name." Capatosto said as he bowed to the chief.

Tyler and Lieutenant Phillips also bowed to the chief and thanked him for the high honor. Tyler wasn't quite sure why only he and Phillips were given the bracelets. Edu explained later when they returned to the fire base.

"Lieutenant is leader and Lam told her husband that you, Sergeant Taylor, had cared for her." Even though Tyler was a specialist, Edu addressed everyone but officers as "sergeant."

After returning to the fire base, Tyler sat in the aid station and thought about his time in Vietnam. Before joining the Civil Affairs Team, he had been either scared or bored to death. This was different. He was helping people who really needed help. It gave him a little insight into what being a doctor must be like. It was so different from being a combat medic, where he barely had time to think about what he was doing and only reacted to the moment. He was starting to believe that maybe Americans were doing some good in this desperate land -- maybe.

Tyler pulled his first night ambush patrol a week later. He had been assigned to the Civil Affairs pretty much on a daily basis, only occasionally pulling guard duty at the fire base. He knew he was probably losing his edge in the jungle but he really didn't miss going out.

There were several new guys on this mission and that made Tyler nervous. He thought it would be his luck to get into a bunch of shit just before he was supposed to go on R&R. He tried to put the bad thoughts out of his head. He had heard from several of the guys who were on their second or third tour that the guys who got it, particularly at the end of their tour, worried way to much about it. He told himself that he had survived "The Hill" and that had to be the worst fight he would ever see.

By the time he pulled himself onto the Huey, he had steadied his nerves and was projecting the confidence of the senior combat medic that he was. They flew out just before sunset and he had to admit that the Central Highlands were beautiful. Then just by thinking the word beautiful, he found himself thinking once again thinking about Patty.

He even wondered if her husband might make it to Nam. Probably not, and being a clerk he wouldn't see any action even if he did. But what if he ended up here? What if he didn't make it back? Would he be there for her? Jesus, he told himself, you don't even know if you'll make it. He settled for just trying to visualize her in his mind when the Huey started its descent. The LZ, as promised in their mission briefing, was the top of a hill that had previously served as a Special Forces outpost. It was just a bare spot in the jungle now. Tyler quickly exited the helicopter and made his way with the rest of the patrol to the edge of the hill, overlooking a lush valley. At least he wasn't climbing mountains this time. They moved out in single file down the slope and after moving into the jungle for an hour, the ambush was set up.

Tyler could see the fear in the faces of the new men as they tried to find a tree or log for cover for the long night ahead. The men settled onto the jungle carpet in silence after the patrol sergeant gave guard assignments for the night, Tyler peered out into the darkness and waited for the dawn. Like many of the nights, nothing happened. It was a relief for Tyler when they finally boarded the Hueys and headed back to the fire base.

"That wasn't too bad was it, Doc?"

One of the new guys, whose name Tyler didn't know, was yelling to him over the whine of the helicopters' rotors. The old Tyler would have said some smart ass thing back, but instead found himself reassuring the rookie infantryman.

"A lot of nights are like that, man. Just keep your edge 'cause it can change real quick out there."

Tyler patted the soldier on the top of his helmet and smiled. The young soldier smiled back as the helicopter rose into the air. One more mission out of the way Tyler thought.

CHAPTER 30

It had been six weeks since Mike Petrov had been blown up at the airport in Saigon. He had endured additional surgery on his broken leg at Camp Zama in Japan. He felt he had been only intermittently conscious during his stay there. Too many drugs floating through his system.

"Hey, Petrov, you know the VA will probably give you some sort of disability payment for your bad lung, man."

Steve Broader had been lying next to Petrov for the last couple weeks at Camp Zama and had evidently decided how he would live off the government for the next 50 years of his life, collecting some sort of disability payments.

"You know, Broader, I would be happy just to get home and out of this fucking hospital."

Petrov tried to ignore Broader and the constant itch of his leg under the cast. It was pure torture.

The doctors at Zama had told him it would heal just fine. It was a different story for his lung. They told him he would never recover full use of it. After six weeks of treatment, he still found it painful to take in a deep breath. He also found out he would not be returning to California to complete his treatment, but instead he would be leaving shortly for Brooke Army Medical Center at Fort Sam Houston in Texas.

Great, he thought, that's where we were supposed to train to be medics -- not Kansas. When he got there he would start to make plans for his future out of the Army. After thinking about it, when his mind wasn't clouded with drugs, he had decided to study civil engineering. Since math was his best subject, he might as well go into something he might be reasonably good at. He figured he could be back in school by next fall. He probably wouldn't be released from the Army until early summer.

He had been allowed to call home a couple times since coming here. His mom seemed distant, but relieved he was going to survive. His dad made some wisecrack about weaving instead of ducking or something like that. He ignored it, knowing he would have to live at home until he could get back on his feet and into school.

Three days later, he was loaded on a MAT transport plane bound for San Antonio, Texas. Good riddance to Asia, he thought.

It was a long flight, but a couple of the nurses were cute and pretty cool. One even provided him with a very thin length of plastic that he was able to slip under his cast and scratch the ever-present itch. He even got a couple cold beers that someone had smuggled aboard the big plane. He wasn't taking as many drugs and his head had cleared enough for some reflection. He found himself wondering about Tyler and Raab. How were they doing? Maybe he was the lucky one. They still had at least six months to try and survive in that insane place. He would be back in school before they would come home.

Brooke Army Medical Center was no picnic. The best thing that happened was the removal of his cast about a week after he arrived. Petrov had been getting around with the aid of crutches and still needed them for his weakened leg. Then he began the rehabilitation phase of his treatment. It wasn't fun. He had to learn how to walk again. There were long hours of weight training to strengthen his mangled leg, which had a long scar where the surgeon had operated on his femur. The feeling was returning, but he still couldn't breathe normally. He seemed to always be out of breath and he wondered what normal would be for him in the future.

The end of the day was best. He was able to soak in a whirlpool bath that relaxed his whole body. He was starting to feel better about his future, and when he saw the condition of many of his fellow soldiers, he felt grateful.

Grateful, he thought about the word. He couldn't remember being that grateful for much of anything before now. He wasn't in Vietnam, he had all his limbs and he actually knew he would be OK. The VA benefits coordinator told him the Army had determined he had a 30 percent permanent disability because of his chest wound. He was also eligible for educational funds under the GI bill. Best of all the Army was discharging him. He started requesting applications from several colleges in California and sent two letters out to his friends in Vietnam.

CHAPTER 31

"Hey, Taylor, I'll trade you a couple cold beers for some good news."

Corporal Andrew Stone peered into the medical aid station as Tyler was examining a bad case of jungle rot on one of the airborne troopers.

Stone was a small black man from Portland, Oregon and served as the company clerk. He always had a cheerful attitude that Tyler was sure coincided with the fact he never had to go out in the field.

"What could be good news in this hell hole, Andy?"

Tyler never looked up from his exam as he spoke. Stone, like most of the cadre around the fire base, knew that only the medics could get ice. It was to keep vaccines cold, but there was usually extra to chill the beer.

"Anyway if it's really good news, you can have one beer," Tyler said, finally looking up at Stone, who was holding some papers.

"Well, my man, you're going to Australia in a couple of weeks," Stone said. "You can get out of the Nam for a while."

Stone handed Tyler a copy of the orders and went to the beer cooler, pulling out a can of Bud.

"I'm sure you don't mind, right? So why Australia? Looking for that white pussy, Taylor?"

Tyler applied some ointment to the soldier's foot and sent him off with a tube of it.

"Try and keep your foot dry and wear clean socks," he said, waiting until the soldier left before answering Stone.

"I am going surfing, Andy. Not a whore hunt. I've seen enough gonorrhea and other crotch rotting diseases here to make me want to go celibate."

Stone laughed and took a swig of his beer.

"That be like you, white boy," he said. " Go to your grave a virgin. Who gives a shit. We'll probably get wasted here anyway."

"I don't think you'll get wasted behind your typewriter, Andy," Tyler replied. "And for the record, I am not a virgin."

Stone laughed again as Tyler retrieved a beer and sat down next to the open door of the tent. A nice breeze was blowing in and he felt good to know he was getting out of here, if only for a little while. Stone pulled up a foot locker and sat on it across from Tyler.

"Yeah, I bet when you were a big stud football player at SC you got lots of pussy."

Tyler smiled and nodded. "That's right, Andy, and look where it got me."

"Well at least you got in college, Tyler." Stone said, the humor draining out of his face. "The only brothers who made it into a good school were the jocks like you. I had the grades out of high school, but no money. I was taking some classes at the community college when I got drafted. There's just no love out there for a small black man."

Tyler leaned over and clicked his beer can to Stone's.

"I love you, Andy. Thanks for the good news."

That night Tyler lay on his cot, surrounded by the ever present mosquito netting. He couldn't sleep and kept mulling over in his mind what R&R in Australia might bring. He had no idea where to surf, how to find a board, he could use, where to stay. No doubt this would be an adventure.

Two weeks later, after a helicopter ride to Cam Ranh Bay from Pleiku, he found himself with a 100 or so other soldiers, all anxious to board a commercial airliner to Australia. While waiting for their flight, Tyler decided to see if anyone was interested in going surfing.

"Anyone want to go surfing?" he loudly yelled out inside the hangar.

He wasn't sure he would get any reply, knowing that most of the men there were interested in drinking and screwing. He was ready for a solo outing when a soldier walked up to him and introduced himself.

Doug Mare was with the 4th Infantry and was stationed around Dak To, when he wasn't humping the jungles. He lived in San Diego and really wanted to go surfing in Australia, but didn't want to go alone. The two soldiers quickly agreed to team up.

While on the plane, Tyler found that Doug knew even less than he did about where to go when they got there.

"The only place I ever really heard about was from the Beach Boys song "Surfin' USA" where they mention Narrabeen, when they're singing about surfing spots," he said. "I remember looking it up because I had never heard the name before. I thought it was some secret Northern California beach. Instead I found it was somewhere in Australia. What's that got to do with surfing in the USA. ... Anyway that might be a starting point."

"Sounds good to me." Tyler replied and went back to trying to find anything he could in an old surfing magazine. If it wasn't giving him any insight to Australia's surfing, it was at least getting him in the mood to be in the water.

"All right, men, you are here as guests of the Australians," an obnoxious sergeant said. "Try to remember that. There were a lot of them who didn't want us here, so they're hoping most of you stay in Kings Cross. That's where we'll drop you off today. It has all the booze and women you want. If you decide to travel around, you are free to do so. Just remember to be right back here in seven days or you'll be AWOL. This isn't Canada, so don't get any ideas about any sanctuary."

The sergeant went on for several minutes about the rules, but nobody was paying attention The soldiers were told to change into their civilian clothes and a short while later were dropped off at the Chevron Hotel, Kings Cross, New South Wales.

After checking into a shared hotel room, Tyler took off looking for a phone to call home. He agreed to meet Doug later at the hotel bar.

Tyler had no idea what time it was in Newport Beach, so he wasn't surprised his dad sounded half asleep when he finally answered the phone.

"Oh my God ,Tyler, it's so good to hear your voice," his dad said, coming to life. "How are you, son?"

Tyler could hear his dad speaking to someone else. Somebody was in bed with him.

"Who's there with you, Dad?"

"Well it's your mother, Tyler. We've decided to give it another try. We were waiting to talk with you about it. A letter didn't seem quite right son."

"Oh" was all Tyler managed to say.

He had been receiving letters from both his parents. There was no mention of any type of reconciliation.

"So how did this happen?" he finally asked.

"It's a long story, son, but I want you to know we're both happy and can't wait for you to get home," his dad said. "Your mom wants to talk to you."

"Tyler, oh I miss you." Tyler could tell she was crying. "It sounds so terrible there. I read the papers and watch the nightly news hoping to see you."

"Well I am OK now, Mom," Tyler said. "I'm going to surf here in Australia. I just got here and wanted to call you know. How are you? Are you and dad happy?"

There was a long pause on the line before his mother answered.

"Tyler, I made a grave mistake leaving your dad," she said. "It was selfish and very juvenile. Maybe someday when you hit your 40s, you'll understand. I just want you to know how much I love him ... and you."

"I am glad for both of you, Mom," Tyler said, a lump growing in his throat. "Please stay happy."

Tyler talked for another 10 minutes before softly replacing the receiver on its hook. He took in a deep breath. He felt like he hadn't been breathing throughout their conversation. He promised he would call again before he returned to Nam. He wasn't sure how to feel. His mom had hurt his father so deeply when she left. Maybe that's what he did to Patty, he thought. If things were different, would she ever take him back? He just wasn't sure how he felt about all of this. Allow yourself to be happy, he told himself.

When he finally found Doug in the crowded bar, he wasn't alone. He had two girls with him and they warmly welcomed his arrival.

"I told you he was good looking, Ann," Doug said, motioning for Tyler to take a seat. Doug had evidently picked out the other girl as his "date." Ann looked up with soft brown eyes at Tyler.

"Nice to meet you, Tyler," she said with a heavy Aussie accent and extended her hand to him.

Doug leaned in and introduced the other girl as Elaine.

"Doug was just telling us that you were both from Southern California. Do you know any actors, Tyler?" Elaine asked as she shook Tyler's hand. "Doug said he didn't know any. I just love Frankie Avalon. He's a surfer, isn't he?"

Tyler grinned. "I am not sure he really surfs, Elaine. But in answer to your question. I don't know any actors. I think they all live in Hollywood. I live at the beach."

A waiter arrived just in time to discourage any more talk about actors. Tyler ordered bourbon with a beer chaser. He hadn't been really drunk in a long time.

After the second round, the thought of being with a hooker started sounding like a better idea. Ann wasn't half bad looking and it had been a long time since he had made love to anybody.

Doug had been telling the girls about their surfing plans before Tyler had arrived. Neither knew much about surfing, but they did know about Narrabeen Beach.

"It's about 20 kilometers from here, north I think," Ann said when Tyler asked her about it. She was drinking Scotch at a good clip. Probably gets a kickback from the bar, Tyler thought. What the hell, he had plenty of money. He had his dad send a money order for a thousand bucks from his savings and he had another five hundred he had saved from his pay. Should be enough for a week, he reasoned.

"I am sure you can rent surfboards there," she said. "You can get a bus out to there; a cab if you have a lot of quids."

Tyler figured quids had something to do with money. He was learning the Aussies use a lot of slang. And he thought this was an English-speaking country!

After their third drink, the girls suggested going to another bar where they could dance. It sounded like a good idea. Tyler was really feeling the drinks and it dawned on him that he hadn't eaten in some time.

"Let's get some dinner first," he said. "Do you guys know a good place? I feel like steak or some of your lobster ... or both."

They all piled into a cab and headed to Sydney's waterfront. Both girls assured Tyler that was where he would find a good restaurant. They ended up at a nice looking place called "Mac's" that had a great view of the harbor.

They dined on lobster and Tyler got his steak on the side. It was wonderful. It had been six months since he had a decent meal. The local wine was surprisingly good. It was called Penfolds Shiraz and Tyler savored its rich flavor, especially with his steak. He thought of his best friend, Tim Rowe. He would really like this.

Tyler was starting to mellow out for the first time since he arrived in Vietnam.

"So do you guys think you can still dance with all this food in you," Ann asked between bites of the bread pudding she had ordered for dessert.

"Hey, we're surfers and we can party all night," a slightly drunk Doug answered with a wide grin.

Before leaving, Doug and Tyler each had a cigar out on the patio of the restaurant. Tyler was sipping cognac while Doug had another glass of wine. The girls had run off to the bathroom.

"So has anybody mentioned a price for their services tonight?" Tyler asked Doug between puffs on his cigar.

"What are you talking about?" Doug said with a quizzical look. "Did you think they were hookers Tyler?"

"I just met them at the bar while I was waiting for you. They were just looking for some fun too. Elaine told me all the Aussie guys care about is drinking and gambling. They wanted someone who would pay them some attention. So buddy, this is not a sure thing you know."

Tyler felt a little embarrassed. The only thing he said was "Oh shit."

When Ann and Elaine returned he was looking at them in a completely different light. They were laughing at some private joke and Tyler really looked at Ann for the first time. She was about 5' 6 and had a nice body. Her eyes had been the first thing he had noticed and now they were even more appealing. She had long brown hair and her dress fit her like a glove. It was funny how his whole outlook changed. Now the warm feelings from the food and drink now expanded to encompass her.

He had known immediately why Doug had gone for Elaine. She had the long blonde hair and blue-green eyes Californians associated with surfer girls. He might have done the same thing had he met them first, but now he was glad he had ended up with Ann. From their conversations during dinner, it was evident she was the brighter of the two. And he had always been attracted to smart women.

The rest of the night was almost a blur. They found a club not far from the restaurant. The live band was pretty good and they played a lot of surf music. It was well after midnight when Doug took Tyler aside.

"I am going with Elaine to her place, so the room is yours, buddy," he said. "I'll see you in the morning and we can try and find Narrabeen."

Elaine said something to Ann and quickly exited the club with Doug.

"Well I guess it's just the two of us, big guy," Ann said when he rejoined her. "Any ideas?"

All the dancing and cutting down on the drinking had sobered Tyler up somewhat.

"How about a nightcap at my hotel , Ann?"

She smiled and took his hand.

"Lead the way, handsome."

He kissed her for the first time in the back of the cab on the way back to the Chevron. She responded very positively and the cab driver had to announce twice that they had arrived at their destination.

She strongly held onto his arm as they entered the hotel.

"Tyler, why don't we have that nightcap in your room," she said.

A knock on the door woke him. Light was streaming into the room and he had to look around to remember where he was and that Ann was asleep next to him. After finding his underwear he went to the door. Doug was standing there with a large grin on his face.

"You going to sleep all day or go surfing?" he asked.

Tyler checked his watch and was surprised it was almost noon. He could hear Ann stirring behind him.

"Give us a little time, Doug," Tyler said. "I'll meet you down in the restaurant."

Doug gave a knowing nod and left. Tyler heard the shower going in the bathroom. He collected the rest of his clothes from the floor and got dressed. He was happy he didn't have a hangover. It had been a wonderful night with Ann. She was a good and caring lover. It was just what Tyler needed after living a near celibate life since arriving in Nam.

He knocked on the bathroom door after the shower stopped and Ann popped her head out of the door.

"Go away, I don't have any makeup on."

She smiled broadly, looking beautiful, he thought. She gave him a quick kiss.

"Doug's downstairs," Tyler said. "Want to meet us there when you're done? I need some coffee."

She agreed, gave him another kiss and retreated into the bathroom. He found Doug attacking a plate of pancakes and bacon when he entered the restaurant.

"Well good morning, Tyler. Sleep well?" Doug asked, arching an eyebrow.

"Like a baby," Tyler answered as he sat down at the table. "So what's the plan, Doug?"

"Elaine had to go to work and I was kicked out of her house early. I found we could take a bus to Narrabeen and save some money. A cab would be a little pricey. The manager here suggested we stay at the Royal Hotel; it's close to the beach. He also said we should be able to rent boards there."

"Shit ,Doug, I am impressed," Tyler said. "And all this while I slept."

Ann joined them a short time later. After getting her phone number and promising to call when they returned to Sydney, she was ready to go.

"I'll walk you out," Tyler said, slipping his arm around Ann's waist and heading for the front of the hotel. She touched the side of his face and smiled while they waited for a cab.

"I had such a great time with you, Tyler," she said. "I wish you were staying here a little longer. Do call me before you leave. I'd love to spend some more time with you before you have to go back to that dreadful country." Tyler gently kissed her and watched as she disappeared into the Sydney traffic.

CHAPTER 32

The bus to Narrabeen took them right along the coast after turning onto Highway 10. Tyler thought how odd it was to be on the east coast of the Pacific Ocean -- the very same ocean that broke in front of his home in Newport Beach.

The Aussies were never at a loss for odd sounding towns. Their trip took them past Manly and Collaroy and finally into Narrabeen. The town had a large inland lake at the north end and the ocean to the east. They took a cab from the bus station to The Royal Hotel. Tyler decided it had to be the oldest hotel he had ever stayed in. It was late afternoon and they were both tired from the trip and the long night before. Surfing could wait until the morning and a good night's sleep.

They set out to explore the city and find a place for an early dinner. There wasn't a lot to see. Surfing had to be the draw. While walking around, they did find a surf board shop whose owner was only too happy to rent a couple of boards to the Yanks.

"You want to surf at North Narrabeen Beach," he said. "It's the one the Beach Boys sang about you know. They made it one of the most famous beaches in Australia. It's protected from the northeasterly winds and the lagoon emptying into the ocean at the north end of the beach makes for an excellent sand bank. Nice waves, mates."

The guy knew a lot about the beach and surfing, Tyler thought. They listened to him for over an hour as he discussed a lot of the hot surfing spots. Unfortunately, most were several hundred miles away. He gave them a tip on where to eat and agreed to be back in the morning so they could get the boards.

The restaurant was a pub, but it looked welcoming and they were hungry, not having eaten since breakfast. It was early evening, but the pub was already crowded. Doug found a small table at the rear of the pub and motioned for Tyler, who had stopped to examine the bar.

"Jesus, that is an old looking bar," he said as he joined Doug.

The waitress had come up to their table and overheard the comment.

"It was built in 1893, mate," she said. "I think this is the third pub it's been in since then."

She smiled and handed each a menu. "So what are you drinking?"

"What's good?" Tyler asked as Doug looked over his menu.

"Well I recommend the Tooheys beer and you can't beat our meat pie. They make it fresh daily, hon."

"What do you think Doug? Give them both a try."

Doug nodded in agreement and the waitress was off with their order.

The beer was great and the meat pie, just OK. But it did fill them up and that was their major concern. A couple beers later a guy about their age walked over from the bar.

"G'day," he said. "You guys Yanks? We don't get too many of you up here."

The guy sat down without being asked and took a long swig of his beer.

Before Doug or Tyler could answer, he leaned over and shook their hands.

"I am Barry O'Rourke," he said. "Born right here in Narrabeen."

As Tyler leaned over to shake hands he noticed that Terry must have been pumping a few barbells over the years. He was a very muscular young man. He almost crushed Tyler's hand with his grip. His smile revealed several missing teeth, giving him a slightly menacing look.

"Well , Barry, I am Tyler Taylor and this is Doug Mare. And you're right, we are Yanks from California. We're also in the Army and on R&R from Vietnam. Now you know all about us."

"Don't know why a couple of diggers would be here," Barry responded.

"For the surfing, Barry. What's a digger? And do you surf?"

"Once in a while, mates," he said. "What I really like is fishing. Lots of good fishing here too, boys. Yeah, a digger is a soldier."

Barry yelled out for more beers at the waitress. She soon arrived with three more Tooheys.

"I doubt if we'll do any fishing, Barry. We only have a week to raise hell." Doug explained to the now nodding Barry.

"So what's it like over there in Vietnam?" the young Aussie said. "You guys see any action?"

Tyler and Doug told him a little about their units. Neither of them really wanted to discuss Nam. They were there to forget about it.

"You know the good surfing is at the North beach," Barry said, taking their cue to change the subject. "Anyway that's what I am told. something about the sand there. The Sheilas aren't too bad either."

"I have to ask, Barry, what's a Shelia?" Doug said it, but Tyler was also confused with the Australian slang.

"Why it's a woman, a girl. You do have them in the States don't you?"

They both nodded and laughed. "I have to remember that one, Barry."

At some point, they staggered back to their hotel room and settled in for the night. It was a very short night. They had promised to meet the surf shop guy at 7:00 a.m. Two sleepy and hung over Americans were true to their word and were banging on the door of the shop on time.

They had worn shorts over their bathing suits and long sleeve T-shirts. It was none too warm, Tyler thought. This was the beginning of Australia's fall season. After talking with the surf shop owner and converting from Celsius to Fahrenheit, he found that the outside temp was generally in the 70s for April. The water temp was 73. They added wetsuit tops to the board rental. The boards they selected were Bing Surfboards and had been imported from California. The only problem they had now was getting to the beach.

"You know, mates, a couple of my boys will be along shortly and you can hitch a ride with them I suppose," the owner said.

Shortly ended up being another hour. It did give them time to wax the boards. Tyler looked at his reflection in the widow of the surf shop. He had a truck driver's tan. His face and lower arms were dark. The rest of him was pale white. It was the same for Doug and neither had any tanning crème.

The shop owners' boys came by in an old pick-up truck and were willing to give the two Yanks a lift to North Narrabeen Beach. Tyler and Doug rode in the back with the boards. The two Australian surfers were Ted and Sam. They were locals, but had surfed all up and down the east coast.

Sam explained the surfing conditions after they parked the truck at the beach.

"Mostly you get a south swell here with a clean hollow beach break," he said. " It's from the sand build-up. You guys aren't shark biscuits, are you?"

"What's a shark biscuit?" Tyler asked, pulling his board from the truck.

"You know, mate, a new surfer who doesn't know anything. Someone who would try to drop in on your wave and try to steal it from you."

Tyler assured them they weren't newbies and wouldn't be stealing any waves.

"That's good because some of these guys can be pretty territorial," he replied

Tyler nodded. He knew all about "territorial" surfers from California to Hawaii. Now he guessed it was the same problem here in Australia. He was determined to get along; even if it meant moving.

Tyler and Doug moved onto the beach and sat on the sand watching the action. Ted and Sam headed out into the water, joining the other locals.

"When I was in high school, my best friend and I were at the Pipeline trying to get up the courage to get in the water when Jerry Lopez advised us to try someplace else," Tyler said. We didn't realize who he was until a couple years later. We did take his advice and left the beach."

"This doesn't look too bad," he said, looking at the half a dozen surfers already in the water.

Tyler watched as the south swells broke between 3 and 5 feet. It looked like Newport or Huntington Beach in California. It wasn't going to be a problem, even if he did have six months of rust to wash off.

Doug was heading for the water when he first saw her. Since she was the only female surfer out there, she would have been hard to miss. Her hair was long and even wet there was no mistake that it was brown. Tyler could see she knew what she was doing. Tyler watched as she slid into a nice 5 -footer, disappearing into the wave's curl before emerging out the back end. She kicked out and immediately headed for the outside. The other surfers seemed to ignore her. From what he observed, she was probably the best one out there. Maybe she subdued the testosterone in a bunch of macho surfers. He paddled out near her, but far enough away to be polite. After all he had been warned about being a "drop in."

He grabbed a couple nice waves and was amazed how quickly his surf feel came back. After each wave he managed to move a little closer to her. Doug had moved off towards the other surfers and he found himself somewhat alone with her. He finally got up the nerve to say something after a break in the sets found everyone just sitting on their boards.

"Hi, nice waves today huh?" Immediately he thought what a dull line that was.

She at first gave him a disinterested look and turned to look out at the ocean. Then, as if something struck her, she looked back at him and paddled over.

"Did you say something?" She asked and Tyler could see her eyes matched the color of the ocean. She was beautiful.

"I was just commenting on the waves. Nice shape to them."

She looked even harder at him and then smiled.

"You're a Yank," she said. "What are you doing here?"

"I came for the surf on the recommendation of the Beach Boys."

It was Tyler's turn to smile and she returned it.

"Well I knew you weren't a local. They wouldn't be caught dead talking to a Shelia surfer. They don't believe we exist. The little woman should be back at the house chilling the beer for whenever they decide to go home. Aussie men are a pain in the ass."

She paddled over right next to him. "I am Maggie, Maggie O'Rourke," she said, reaching out and shaking Tyler's hand like a man.

"Uh, Tyler Taylor," he replied. He was totally off his game already with this girl, he thought.

"So where are you from Tyler Taylor and why are you really here?"

"Well I live in Newport Beach. That's in California. I am in the Army and I am here on leave from Vietnam."

She nodded. "Too bad for you. I mean being in the Army, not being here or living in Newport Beach, which by the way I've heard about. We are a little familiar with the States you know."

There was an awkward silence between them. It was broken by a new set of waves that they set out to catch. After a couple hours of hard surfing they paddled into the shore. Doug was sitting on the beach next to his board. Tyler could see his eyes widen as he took in Maggie.

"Maggie, this is my friend and travelling companion, Doug Mare."

She shook his hand just like she had with Tyler. When she smiled at Doug, Tyler noted she had perfectly straight white teeth. When she peeled off her wet suit top it completed the picture. She's perfect, Taylor thought.

"Where are you boys staying?" she asked, taking a seat on the sand.

"The Royal Hotel. It's not much, but we have a roof over our head," Tyler said, sitting down beside her. He left his wet suit top on to cover the pale skin.

"I am staying there too," she said. "You know they're tearing it down at the end of the year. New modern hotel is going in."

"So where do you live, Maggie? Sydney?" Tyler asked.

"No, but that's where I've been for the past week," she said. "I am on holiday too. If you want to shop, Sydney's the place. I live in Brisbane. It's way north of here. The real surf is up there. A place called Byron Bay. I am just working my way up the coast and trying other surf spots."

"Oh, a surfing safari," Doug chimed in.

"I guess something like that," Maggie said. "I start back to school in July. I just finished a census, I think you call it a semester in the States. Anyway I go to the University of Queensland in Brisbane. You have to remember you're down under and our seasons are reversed. We're in early fall now, just ending summer."

"So what are you studying?" Tyler asked, becoming was even more interested, if that was possible.

"I am enrolled in pre-law," she said. "Hopefully someday I'll get into law school and become a lawyer. Have you guys been in college?"

Tyler answered that he had been at USC, but skipped over why he was no longer there or anything about football. Doug had never been to college. He had gone to work right out of high school.

The wind had picked up while they were on the beach and most of the surfers had come in. The waves had been blown flat.

"Listen, do you guys want a lift back to the hotel?" Maggie asked.

"Only if we can buy you dinner," Tyler answered immediately.

"I guess I'll be safe with you Yanks," she said. "Why not?"

They all walked up to Maggie's car, which was a '62 Ford station wagon. They stored the boards through the open back window. Tyler sat up front with Maggie and Doug sat in the back seat. He had evidently figured out that Tyler had his sights set on her.

CHAPTER 33

She met him in the lobby of the hotel promptly at seven. She was in a summer dress and if she looked great in a swimsuit, she was now stunning.

"I know a little Italian place you might like, Tyler. By the way, where's Doug?"

"He decided to hang out at the pub with some of the surfers we drove to the beach with today," he said. "Also he met a girl in Sydney he wanted to call tonight. I think he's in love. Oh, and Italian sounds great. I am starved."

The truth was that Tyler had convinced Doug he really needed to be alone with Maggie. That's when he decided to call Elaine.

The restaurant was a short walk from the hotel. He hadn't had any Italian food -- not even pizza -- since landing in Vietnam. They ordered a bottle of Chianti and fried calamari to start. Tyler had polished off most of both by the time his veal parmesan arrived. Maggie had nibbled on a salad and the bread. They exchanged mostly small talk until the second bottle of wine was opened.

"So what is it like in Vietnam, Tyler?" she asked. "Have you been in combat? Have you had to kill anyone?"

Maggie looked intently across the table at the handsome soldier. Tyler took another sip of wine before answering her. He couldn't judge how she might feel about the war. He certainly wouldn't tell her about shooting NVA on the "Hill."

"Lots of questions, Maggie. Well it isn't fun and I can't wait to get out of there. I was drafted or I would never have been in the Army. I was in a lot of fighting when I first got there. It was true horror. We lost a lot of good men and I question what for. I am a combat medic and my job isn't killing people, it's saving them. I've been in and out of combat from the start, but lately it's been pretty quiet. I've been working with the Montagnard tribesman in the Central Highlands of the country. I find that rewarding. They are good people.

"I am so sorry, Tyler," she said. "The stories we hear here are so frightful. Some of our boys are over there. I think somewhere around Saigon."

Her eyes were sad and Tyler really didn't want to go there. He was here to forget the war for a while.

"Tell me more about the Montagnards," Maggie said. "They sound a little like our Aborigines here."

Tyler spent the next hour talking about the Montagnards. It didn't bother him to talk about them. Maggie told him about the interior Aborigine tribes and their "walkabouts."

Time passed so quickly. He told her the truth about how he had been kicked off the football team and eventually left school. How he wanted to return after the Army and finish school and maybe be an architect someday. He shared his football dream and the chance to play again. She was so easy to talk with he even told her about Patty and how he lost her.

Maggie listened intently, asking questions, keeping him loose along with the wine. She told him about Australian men and their lack of romance.

"I doubt if I'll ever get married, Tyler," she said. "I don't want to be a piece of furniture or sports fixture. To be honest, you're the first man, other than my dad, who has cared what I had to say. It's very refreshing. I could get used to it."

Maggie reached across the table and took Tyler's hand. Her smile almost melted him. The moment passed too quickly, interrupted by the waitress clearing her throat. Tyler looked up to see they were the only patrons left in the restaurant.

"I am sorry, sir, but we are closing."

Tyler reached in his pocket for his money.

"Let me help, Tyler," Maggie implored, reaching for her purse.

"Hey, a deal's a deal," he said. "I wouldn't have it any other way, Maggie. This has been the best night I've had in a long time."

"It doesn't have to end yet, Tyler. Let's go back to the hotel and wake up Doug."

They did go back to the hotel, but never saw Doug. In Maggie's room they talked to early morning. She fell asleep next to him after giving him one light kiss. It was after noon before he awoke. Maggie was still asleep when he stood up. She stirred as he entered the bathroom to relieve himself and throw some water on his face. He figured Doug was probably pissed off he missed the morning surfing as planned. It was definitely worth it, he thought. Maggie was up when he came back into the room. She even looked great in the morning.

"Look at me, sleeping in my dress all night," she said. "What must you think?"

"I think you forgot what I said about the night," Tyler replied. "It was the best. I am glad you trusted me to stay with you."

"Well you were a perfect gentleman, I must say. You didn't even try for a kiss."

"Give me a break," he said. "I've been out of practice."

Maggie laughed. "Oh I doubt that, Tyler. No cute Vietnamese girls up there?"

"Trust me, Maggie, when you're a medic and treat all the sexually transmitted diseases, you lose your interest quick."

"Umm," was her only reply.

"I need to check on Doug, then how about a late breakfast or early lunch?"

"That sounds great," she said. "I guess we missed the morning surf, huh? Before you go Tyler, I wanted to ask you something I thought about last night. I am heading North today. Lots of surfing spots between here and Byron Bay. Do you and Doug want to go with me? The only drawback is you would need to fly back from Brisbane to Sydney. It's not too expensive."

She flashed her extremely cute smile, and Tyler was ready to go.

"I would love to, Maggie. Let me check with Doug. I'll meet you in the lobby in say an hour."

"That would be great, Tyler. Right now I need a shower to wake up."

Tyler returned to his room to find it empty. All of Doug's stuff was gone. On his bed was a note:

Tyler,

I called Elaine last night and after talking for a couple hours she asked me to spend the rest of my leave with her. She's going to arrange for some vacation time today. I didn't want to barge in on you and Maggie this morning. I took the bus back to Sydney early today and by the time you read this I'll probably be there. I am sorry that surfing just wasn't that important to me. Maggie seems real fine. Hope it works for you. See you on the plane back.

Doug

P.S. Could you get the wet suit and board back. Thanks!

If he hadn't met Maggie, Tyler would have been a little pissed. After her invitation today, this was perfect. It dawned on him he would have to buy the board or a board he could afford. He sure wouldn't be back here after today. He didn't want to worry about renting boards all the way up the coast. Doug probably did him a favor.

He took a quick shower, packed up his belongings and headed down to the lobby, heading off on what he hoped would be a great adventure.

CHAPTER 34

The surf shop owner was a hard bargainer. Tyler had been negotiating for the Bing surfboard and the very used wetsuit top for the past half hour. Maggie looked anxious to get on the road but said nothing. They finally agreed on $100.

"So we have five days before you need to get on a plane in Brisbane," Maggie announced matter of factly. "I think we'll start our little surfing safari in a place called Newcastle. It's a much better place for an experienced surfer than here. It's only about 50 kilometers, so we can still catch the late afternoon surf."

Maggie pointed the car north up Highway 1. Tyler settled in for the trip.

Newcastle had a lot of surfing beaches to choose from. Maggie explained that one in particular, "The Harbor," was considered the most dangerous beach because of the barrel waves. She suggested they try "The Wedge" which was the most popular.

"You know, Maggie, we have "The Wedge" in Newport Beach but it's a body-surfing spot," he said. "The surf breaks too close to shore for a board, but I've seen 20 foot waves there. By the way, I wasn't in the water."

She had been very quiet during the drive. Tyler wondered if she might be reconsidering her decision to bring him with her. He was, after all, pretty much a stranger. Maybe he was overanalyzing it, he told himself as she parked the car at the beach. Before he could get out she touched him on his shoulder. He turned to face her. She had a serious look on her face.

"There's something you need to know about me, Tyler," she said, gazing steadily into his eyes. "I've been debating whether it was important or not. I've decided it is. I know I just met you but I already know I could really fall for you. I've never been with a man before. "

She blushed and realized she needed to be more specific.

"What I am trying to say is that I am a virgin. I told you last night how I felt about the men around here. I've dated and stuff, just nothing very serious. I'm worried but also excited you could be different. I just thought you should know."

Tyler placed his arms around her and drew her in tight to his body.

"Maggie, we're going to take this one day at a time," he said. "No pressure from me, I promise. I think it's so admirable really."

He held her for a long time before lifting her chin so their lips could meet. She kissed him gently.

"Hey, are we going surfing," Tyler said, breaking the moment for now.

She laughed. "Oh, was that why we're here?"

Tyler untangled from her and opened the car door. They removed the boards and got into their wet suits. On the beach, as was Tyler's custom at any new beach, he watched the waves, learning their personality.

What he saw were big clean swells. Maggie was already heading out. He caught up to her on the outside. She was a true surfer, he thought. Once in the water she was no longer fragile or concerned. She was a surfer who knew what she was doing. In her element, he kept thinking -- just like he was. He looked around at the sea. It was the same Pacific Ocean that broke on his home beach in California. So immense he thought.

He looked over in time to see Maggie take off on a nice right break. He lost sight of her as she dropped down into the curl. She wasn't waiting for any guy to lead the way. He thought back to their conversation in the car. He would never push her -- never.

"Jesus," he thought. "What if she was the one. How impossible would that be. Was there any place further away than Australia? Shit, Tyler, think about it, you still have another five months to survive in the Nam. This no time to get all serious about a girl, even if she is a great surfer, beautiful and smart."

Maybe he was just looking for someone to move Patty over from the center of his heart. This really wasn't what he thought he'd be thinking about on his third day of R&R.

A great wave loomed behind him and he paddled hard to catch it. He dropped way too quick into the break and soon found himself rolling along the bottom. At least there were no rocks here. He finally broke the surface gasping for air and feeling very alive.

He found his board almost on the beach. By the time he had paddled out again, Maggie had caught another wave and was already back outside. She smiled broadly at him.

"Having a little trouble with our Aussie waves, Tyler?"

"Ah, it was a little small for me," he said. "I couldn't get used to the slow speed of it. You know they're much faster in my end of the world."

It was his turn to smile now. She just shook her head and said, "I am sure they are, Deary. Try and keep up with me this time."

And he did. They took off together on the next wave. It was fun to share and they managed not to crash into each other.

They surfed until sunset, then made their way back to the car after rinsing off with a hose near a restroom on the beach. She changed in the back seat while Tyler kept guard. He was proud he didn't even attempt a sneaky look. He pulled off his wet suit on the side of the road and changed into a pair of Levi's and a T-shirt.

"So here's my plan, Tyler," she said after he had put the boards away and joined her in the car. She had on shorts and a sleeveless blouse. She had pulled her wet hair back into a pony tail and as usual looked hot.

"We have a long ride to Byron Bay tomorrow if we want to stay here. We'll lose a day of surfing. What do you think about driving all night or at least until we can't keep our eyes open. We could take turns driving and sleeping. We could stop for dinner in Port Macquarie, then keep going."

"I think that sounds good. My only concern is my stomach. As usual I am starved."

"We'll get some snacks to hold you over. I need some more petrol too."

Maggie leaned over any kissed him again. This time hard, her tongue exploring his. Just as quickly she pulled away and started the car.

"Time to hit the road."

Dinner ended up to be three hours later in Port Macquarie. It was a good thing Tyler had bought plenty of nuts, chips and Cokes to snack on. He was beginning to believe Maggie ran on air, but she surprised him at dinner. They both had steak and lobster and she cleaned her plate. Tyler avoided drinking, as it was his turn to drive.

"It's about 6 hours from here to Byron Bay," Maggie said, sipping her wine. "It will be late when we get there. Should I make some reservations? I know a nice place on the beach I think you would love."

Tyler agreed immediately. It made it easier for him. Would she book two rooms or one? He guessed he would find out soon enough.

She fell asleep almost immediately after getting him back to Pacific Highway. It was a no brainer from there, just keep going north and stay on the road. He drove along in the darkness and thought about Vietnam. He hated the thought of going back there. He hated the jungle, the bugs, the malaria, the rain. When he thought about it, there was nothing he really liked about being there. He had a fleeting thought of just staying here with Maggie, but knew he wouldn't. No matter what happened, he needed to go all the way to the end.

It was almost 3 in the morning by the time he pulled into Byron Bay. Maggie had slept the entire time and Tyler was beat. He regretted having to wake her, but he had no idea where the Beach Hotel was. She just looked so damn cute sleeping.

"Oh, Tyler, I didn't mean for you to drive the whole way," Maggie said. "You should have woke me up."

She stretched and yawned at the same time, then looked out the window, got her bearings and directed Tyler to the hotel, where they had to wake up a sleeping clerk to get the room. The hotel was right on the beach and even in the dark, Tyler could make out the waves in the moonlight. The beach looked beautiful and he was pleasantly surprised to find the room only had one large bed. It was really a suite as opposed to a room. It had a nice sitting area, a small refrigerator and a deck that looked out on the ocean. The bathroom was very large by hotel standards and had a shower and separate soaking tub; big enough for two.

He retrieved their luggage from the car and by the time he returned Maggie was in the bed. She was wearing a T-shirt and underpants. Not exactly sexy, but she still looked great. He undressed in the bathroom, matching her attire.

"I bet you're tired?" Maggie said a little nervously.

"You're right, girl. Very tired."

Tyler pulled back the sheets and slid into the bed. He rolled on his side and faced her. She gently reached over and cupped his head pulling him next to her. She kissed him again like she had done earlier in the car. He felt a lot of passion and he sensed if he wanted to, it could go further. He pushed her head away and held her at shoulder length.

"Believe me, Maggie, I want you, but you need to think about this before we take the next step. Right now I can't be a long term possibility and I don't want you to regret anything after I leave. We still have some time. Let's see how you feel tomorrow."

Tyler once again cradled her head on his chest, felt proud of himself and fell asleep.

CHAPTER 35

The bright sunlight streamed into the room and, although Tyler had only slept six hours, he woke refreshed. His first thought was how amazing it was to be here. He heard Maggie in the shower. He looked out onto the beach and it looked even better than the night before. He was anxious to get into the water again.

He pulled on his swimsuit and a pair of shorts and decided to wear the same T-shirt he had slept in. Clean clothes were becoming limited. He did a quick count of his remaining funds and found he still had over $800. We are in good shape, he thought.

Maggie emerged from the bathroom and sat down on the edge of the bed.

"How did you sleep, Tyler?"

"Great, and you?" he said, winking at her.

"I had a little trouble falling back to sleep for a couple reasons," she said.

Tyler politely didn't question further, saying only, "How about a little breakfast before we hit the surf?"

They found a little cafe and settled in with what looked like locals.

"So would you like to know about this little beach town?" Maggie asked between bites of toast she had smeared with some black smelly spread she identified as Vegemite. Tyler settled for pancakes and sausage.

"For sure." Tyler responded, using a little surf jargon he didn't think Maggie got.

"Well for thousands of years the Aboriginal tribes came here to trade goods and find mates," she said. "Captain James Cook found the place around 1770 and named it after a guy named John Byron, who was another famous sailor.

"It's been primarily an industrial town, from logging to whaling, since then. The smell from all the meat and dairy farms along with the annual slaughter of whales was appalling so most people avoided it. The place kind of shut down in the late '50s, until the surfers discovered it in the last 10 years, now it's turning into a tourist destination. I have to show you the old lighthouse, it's really cool. It was built in about 1900."

"This is great, Maggie. I was thinking this morning how unbelievable it was to be here and to have met you. I haven't felt this good in a long time. It's not the surfing; it's you."

Tyler reached over and took Maggie's small hand in his.

"Jesus, I wish some things were different for me right now."

Maggie gripped his hand with both of hers.

"Tyler, what we have is today," she said. "Neither of us knows what the future might bring. Let's enjoy what God has given us. By the way I haven't felt this good either for a long time, maybe ever."

They spent the rest of the morning surfing at a spot called "The Wreck." It was aptly named because of a shipwreck lying on the beach. It had a point break, but wasn't all that challenging. The Main Beach had better swells and was close to their hotel.

The water was a little warmer here than in Narrabeen and the sun was warmer. Tyler decided he could really fall in love with this small surfing town. They had lunch at a little cafe on the beach. After ordering, Tyler wandered off to find a bathroom, leaving Maggie to her own thoughts.

She was really falling for this handsome American soldier. She let the word love float around her head. Could she be in love with someone she just met? Her parents had a one month romance before they got married and had been together for over 30 years now. Did it always happen that fast? She didn't know the answer. What she did know was he made her feel special, very special. She didn't want to let him go and she wanted to give herself to him.

She was still thinking when he slid into the booth next to her.

"Penny for your thoughts," Tyler said as he took a sip of his beer.

"What?" Maggie said, jolted from her deepest thoughts.

"I guess it's an American term: Penny for what you're thinking. You know, you looked to be so distant."

"Oh, I was thinking when we go to Brisbane I would like you to meet my parents," Maggie said. "I think they would really like you."

"Really, that would be great. I'd like to meet them and see where you grew up."

They ended up surfing just below the lighthouse, at a place the locals called "Wategos." It proved to be a big challenge. There was a combination reef-sand break that produced slow rights. The view from the ocean was spectacular. It only reinforced Tyler's decision that sometime he would return. He already had one good reason.

When the wind came up in the early afternoon, they decided to explore the lighthouse. Byron Bay Lighthouse sat on a cliff overlooking the Pacific. It reminded Tyler of ones he had seen on the Oregon Coast. By the time they reached it, the wind had really picked up and the temperature was dropping. The lighthouse wasn't open for touring and Tyler found himself just staring at the sea and the beautiful girl who was now snuggling against him. It looked like a storm was coming in.

The rain had just started to fall when they entered the Beefy Monkey Restaurant, Bar and Dance Hall.

"I do hope you dance Tyler, because I love to," Maggie said, pulling him into the bar. A live band was playing loud surf music.

"I'll give it a try, Maggie, but first let's get something to eat."

They munched on cheeseburgers. Maggie ate about half of hers and then passed the rest over to Tyler who was glad to get it. He wondered what this girl ran on.

"If it's raining again tomorrow would you like to move on to Brisbane?" she said. "We could spend the night at my folks and I could show you around before you have to leave on Monday."

"You sure they would want a strange American staying at their home?" Tyler asked after starting on his second beer. If he was going to dance he needed to loosen up a little.

"Oh they will love you, Tyler. Besides it is a big place."

"So what do your folks do?"

"Well my dad owns a construction company and my mom is a homemaker. How about yours?"

Tyler realized he really hadn't said anything about his parents. He had laid out almost everything else to her. Why not them?

"Well my dad's an architect . My mom's another story. She was a nurse and now she's a artist, I guess."

Tyler explained his parents' separation, her journey to Big Sur, the boyfriend and eventual return to his father. He realized the story was still hard to tell -- to anyone.

His downcast eyes must have told the story to Maggie. She reached over and gently patted his arm.

"Come on, let's see if your dance moves are as good as your surfing."

Maggie pulled him up from the table and maneuvered him out to the dance floor. It was almost 1 in the morning by the time they headed back to their room.

"You're not a bad dancer either."

Maggie slapped him on the butt as they walked along the beach. It just seemed so right to be with her, Tyler thought. Why did she have to live a world apart from him? Would this be their last night alone? If they went to her parents tomorrow, there would be little chance of sleeping together. It wasn't sex, he had already made the decision on that. It wasn't going to happen. Vietnam still loomed like some dark cloud out there. He had always wanted to survive it, but now more than ever. Someday he would see her again. He had to.

That night their lovemaking went way beyond their two other nights together. She was a little drunk and wanted to go all the way. He gently assured her it was better for them to wait. They managed to release some of their passion without Maggie losing her virginity. The next morning they woke to the rain falling heavily on the roof of their hotel room. She lay naked in his arms.

"I want to see you again, Tyler. I love you."

Tyler looked into the eyes of the woman he imagined he could spend the rest of his life with.

"Oh, Maggie, I have been so lost and now I have found what I have always wanted," Tyler said. "I love you too."

CHAPTER 36

Brisbane was a much larger city than Tyler had imagined. Maggie pointed out the sights as she effortlessly maneuvered through the city streets.

"It's the third largest city in Australia and has over a million people," she said.

Tyler was interested in the distinctive architecture in many of the areas they drove through.

"The style is called Queenslander and a lot of the streets are named after the Royals. You'll see it even closer, my parents home was built in that style. I've noticed that you have a keen interest in architecture; is that because of your father?"

"Well I think I told you, I had architecture as my major at USC," Tyler said. "I've been thinking that I would like to be one someday. I can go back to school next year. I am might be eligible for a early separation from the Army and could conceivably be back in school by this fall. The big question is whether they will let me back into the program. I didn't leave under the best of circumstances, as I told you. Then the next question is what do I do about you?"

Maggie was still trying to watch the traffic in front of her, but glanced over at him.

"Well I have always wanted to see the States and being a surfer, perhaps I would start in say ... Southern California. It could be my graduation gift from the folks. I'll be finished at least with my undergrad degree this year. How would that be for a start?"

Tyler looked over at her. She was smiling broadly.

"I think that would be perfect, Maggie."

They drove along the Brisbane River for several miles before turning into a gated drive that marked the beginning of an enclave of homes above the river. It reminded Tyler of pictures he had seen of New England homes.

Maggie pulled into the driveway of a home near the end of the street. As promised it was a large Queenslander style home with a large verandah wrapped around the entire front of the house. The main entrance was reached by two grand staircases that connected into a single staircase. The homes had been built in this style for ventilation and to protect them from river flooding, Maggie explained. There was a turret at the corner of the house, and lots of palm trees landscaped the property.

"This is called Federation style, but I am not sure why," she said. "Maybe it's the turret."

Tyler was starting to step from the car just as a large black lab bolted from somewhere in the backyard. Maggie jumped out to meet the energetic dog, which looked extremely pleased to see her.

"Jake, you good dog. Come here."

Jake dismissed Tyler and ran to his owner. While Jake smothered Maggie with dog kisses, Tyler noticed a woman on the verandah looking down at them. He waved, assuming it was Maggie's mom. She waved back and started down the stairs.

"Hello, Tyler, I'm Sally."

Maggie's mom shook hands with Tyler and, before he could say anything, she turned to hug her daughter. Tyler thought she was a very attractive woman. She appeared to be maybe 10 years older than his own mom. She turned back toward Tyler, still holding her daughter close to her.

"So you're the Yank that has stolen my baby's heart."

Tyler blushed, unsure what to say.

"Mom, look what you've done," Maggie said. "Now he's embarrassed."

They all laughed. Tyler gathered up their luggage and they headed towards the house.

"Well , Mrs. O'Rourke, the truth is, she stole my heart first," he finally said. "Thank you so much for inviting me into your home. I am sure it must be awkward."

"Well first of all, Tyler, as I told you my name is Sally. Mrs. O'Rourke is my mother-in-law. I don't want to feel any older than I am. Second, we are thrilled to have you here since you are the first lad Maggie has ever brought home for us to meet. I think that is pretty special. Now come up, I've made some lunch for us. Maggie's dad won't be home until later. He's at work, but is anxious to meet you too.

Sally O'Rourke placed her arm around Tyler's shoulder and hugged him. He was starting to see where Maggie got her warmth.

They dined on grilled white fish and drank beer. After lunch Maggie took him to a room, next to hers, that had been her older brother's. She had told him about her two older brothers who had tortured her until they both moved to Sydney. "Typical Aussie men," was how she described them. He didn't bother unpacking since .... he had to leave tomorrow. Maggie helped him with reservations for plane back to Sydney. He had to report by 1800 hours, so he took the latest flight possible. The rest of the afternoon he explored the property around the O'Rourke residence with Maggie. They sat on the bank of the Brisbane River and talked about the future -- their future.

"I will write you whenever I get a minute," Tyler said. "I just want you to understand that sometimes it's impossible to write when I am out in the field. There's not many mailboxes in the jungle. It's pretty wet

Try to Remember ... Vietnam   193

out there too. And I know this is hard to hear, but darling if anything happens to me, I'll make arrangements that you will be notified."

Maggie started to cry. "Tyler, nothing can happen to you, my love. God would not be that cruel. I just found you and you have to come back to me."

Tyler held her for a long time as they watched the river roll by. It was so tranquil, but he was starting to feel the acid churn in his stomach as he thought about returning to the jungle. He had a ways to go and who knew what might happen there. Shit, he thought, get back to today and quit thinking about tomorrow. He was so deep in his thoughts that he was startled by the voice from behind him: "I thought I might find you down here."

Tyler and Maggie turned to see a large man with a wide grin on his face bounding down the hill.

"Dad!" Maggie exclaimed, jumping up and running to her father. He picked her off the ground in a tight bear hug.

Maggie grabbed her father's hand and pulled him down to Tyler.

"Dad, this is Tyler Taylor. Tyler, this is my dad, Pat."

The men shook hands and looked each other over.

"Well welcome, Tyler," Pat O'Rourke said after a moment. "I am sorry you have to leave so soon. My wife told me your flight was tomorrow. I was hoping we could get to spend a little more time together, but I hear my daughter has been showing you all our secret surf spots."

It turned out that Mr. O'Rourke was a surfer in his own right. It gave him and Tyler an immediate topic of discussion. Tyler told him of all the spots they had surfed during the week.

"You know, Pat, I had to buy a board. It's way too big for Maggie and it wouldn't do me much good in Vietnam, so I'd like you to have it."

Tyler could tell that he was touched by the gesture.

"I am sure we can put it to use, Tyler. Thank you so much. I think my wife wanted us to head back. She has a big dinner planned.

Once back at the house, Pat poured a shot of scotch for both of them. They sat in the living room. Maggie had joined her mother in the kitchen. The smell of a wonderful dinner drifted through the house. Pat took out a pipe and lit it, adding the smell of tobacco to that of the cooking. They watched the evening news and all of a sudden Tyler welled up inside. This was what he had missed so much. The sense of family and well-being that came with it. He hoped this would all return for his own family and that his mom's midlife crisis was over. A news clip of fighting in Vietnam came on the program. Both men watched in silence.

"Pretty bad over there, son?" Pat asked with sad eyes.

"It is a hard place to define, Pat. One day it's all fighting, then you can go for weeks with nothing happening. I guess the hardest part is the uncertainty of what will happen next. That's what tears you up. Well that and seeing your friends killed or wounded."

"Have you lost a lot of friends, Tyler?"

"When I first got there we were in a horrible fight near Dak To," he replied. "I hadn't been there long enough to know the guys well. We lost a lot of men. Just before I came here one of my closest friends was severely wounded in Saigon during the Tet offensive. The only good thing about it is he's back home healing. You learn not to make real close friends there. It hurts too hard when you lose them."

Pat grabbed the scotch bottle and poured them each another drink.

"I was too young for World War II and too old for this one," Pat said. "I have never experienced anything like you're going through. I watch the news and just shake my head at the waste of fine young men like yourself. Do you think any of this is going to make a bit of difference down the road?"

Tyler thought about that for a while and sipped on the scotch. He had never liked it in the past, but tonight it tasted good.

'We could win over there, but not the way we're fighting the war now," he said finally. "I hate to say it, but I think in the end we'll lose."

Up to that point Tyler had never vocalized how he felt. After all he was a paratrooper, one of the best. Talk like that was for losers. That's what the lifers would say, and yet sometimes he wondered what they really thought privately.

The women returned to the room and interrupted the conversation. Both were carrying wine glasses and evidently had not missed happy hour. Maggie had heard a little of their talk.

"Dad, now don't just talk about the war," she said. "Tyler has a lot of interesting stories that have nothing to do with being a soldier. You know he played football, well the American style, at the University of Southern California. And he would like to be an architect one day. You guys could talk about building stuff, but right now I am calling you both for dinner."

After an amazing meal of lamb from New Zealand, with all the side dishes you could ask for, Sally served homemade ice cream. Tyler had two bowls and was embarrassed to ask for more, when Sally filled his bowl again. The sense of family once again welled up in him. These were wonderful, warm, loving people.

Pat broke out his oldest bottle of cognac after the dishes had been cleared.

"We're going to have ours out on the verandah," Maggie said. "Dad, you can help mom with the dishes. I want him to myself for a while."

They took their cognac and retreated to the porch swing. They sat their staring out at the stars, swinging like a couple kids.

"Your parents are great, Maggie. You're very lucky to have them. I think you'll like mine when you meet them. My mom always said she would have loved to have had a daughter."

Several hours later they were still on the verandah when Sally came out to say they were going to bed. Maggie stood up and hugged her mom. Then Tyler did too.

When they finally made their way to bed, Maggie pulled them into her room for their last night. It was one he would never forget. He was back in his own bed next door before anyone stirred, he just didn't sleep.

The next day she drove him to the airport and watched tearfully as he boarded the plane. It tore him up to say goodbye, but he knew that he would replay this week again and again. He knew he would see her in California, he told himself, as he settled into a seat and watched as Brisbane disappeared behind him.

CHAPTER 37

John Raab realized that after the last week in the jungle, he was exhausted. There had been no contact with the enemy. No one was killed or even injured. It was the constant stress and anticipation that wore you thin. It dawned on him that he no longer laughed at anything. He couldn't think of anything that was funny. He had tried so hard to go to his spiritual side; it seemed blocked.

When he finally got a shower and a clean set of fatigues on, he opened his mail that had been left for him at Tuy Hoa. A letter from Tyler about his impending R&R to Australia to surf. That was Tyler he thought, getting back in the water. Maybe he needed to get back in the water in another way. He was eligible to go on R&R. He had almost decided not to even go. What would he do in any of those countries? Drinking and sex were the main attraction for the soldiers he knew. He wasn't interested in either. It wasn't like he wouldn't like to be with a woman, just not some Asian whore. He was thinking more on the lines of Chris Rowe, like that would ever happen.

One of the chaplains had told him about visiting Thailand and the wonderful temples and sights outside of Bangkok. Raab had come to admire the work of the Buddhist monks he had seen in Saigon and in the Central Highlands. Maybe he should get away for a while. The next morning after thinking about it all night, he made a formal request for R&R in Thailand.

Three weeks later Raab found himself in the sweltering heat of Bangkok. It was more humid than Vietnam and he was wondering if he had made a wise decision. After some research he had decided to go to Chiang Mai in the northern part of Thailand. He had his taxi drive him to the Hua Lamphong railway station and, after finally finding an agent who spoke English, he learned the train left in the late evening and the trip took about 12 hours. The agent urged him to book his passage in a private car that had a bed and was air conditioned. It seemed like good advice. After leaving the train station he checked into a nearby hotel. It was nearly 12 hours until the train left and he felt like a swim, some food and a nap.

Raab dove into the pool and felt the cool water relax his tense body. He completed about 20 laps of the pool before pulling himself out and onto a deck chair. A waiter brought him a Coke and it dawned on him that for the first time in seven months, no one around him was carrying a gun. It was a good feeling. What did he want to take away from this journey, he asked himself. It finally dawned on him: He wanted to find his old self again.

He slept fitfully after a meal of a broth with noodles and pieces of chicken and vegetables. It was almost midnight by the time he returned to the railway station. Raab was impressed with the style of the old building. A pamphlet he found inside identified it as Italian Neo-Renaissance. It had a wooden roof and stained glass windows. It wasn't what he expected to find in Bangkok.

The train left shortly after he settled into his small private berth. He sat at the window and watched as Bangkok disappeared and they headed out into the countryside. The rhythm of the train made him sleepy and he was out shortly after falling fully clothed into the small bed. Raab dreamed of violent combat, being lost alone in the jungle and the many dead soldiers he had seen over the past seven months. He woke once with a start, trying to locate his .45 pistol, only to eventually realize where he was. He must have slept soundly the remainder of the night because sunlight was finally breaking through the rain clouds when he woke. He checked his wristwatch and found it was almost 10 in the morning. It was the longest he could remember sleeping since leaving home.

He had some steamed rice and tea in the dining car and watched the scenery go by. The area was similar to Vietnam. Lots of jungle and mountains. About 3 in the afternoon the train pulled into Chiang Mai. Raab was now some 400 miles from Bangkok. He didn't expect to see too many American soldiers here. In fact he would see none.

Chiang Mai is the largest city in northern Thailand. It is located on the Ping river which is a major tributary of the Chao Phraya River. Raab wandered around and noted nothing cosmopolitan about it. The city, which existed because of its strategic location on an ancient trade route, had over 300 Buddhist temples.

He wasn't sure what to do first. As he wandered the streets and noted that the preferred mode of transportation was the small motorbikes that were also popular with the locals in Vietnam. He thought about renting one, but decided against it in light of the heavy traffic and his inexperience in driving anything, let alone a motorbike.

Raab found himself, quite by accident, at the gate of the Dokmai Garden. He signed up for a tour with the only English-speaking guide they had. He was fascinated with the more than 600 plant species and food markets. He bought some local fruit and munched on it as the guide pointed out the highlights.

it was late afternoon when the tour concluded. The guide, whose name was Bahn, talked at length with Raab at the park's exit.

"You should go to the temples, sir, they are so beautiful. You can also take an elephant into the jungle. Very exciting, sir!"

"I've seen plenty of jungle, Bahn. Can you point me in the direction of a temple I could tour?"

"Of course, sir. The most famous temple is Wat Phrathat Doi Suthep," he said. "It is just north of here. Also you must see Wat Chiang

Man. It is our oldest temple. You can see the marble and crystal Buddha there. There are many others to see."

After leaving the park Raab decided to put off seeing any temples and instead find a place to spend the night. It had started raining again and the heat was oppressive. So much for his thought that the north might be cooler than Bangkok. He flagged down a tuktuk, a little moped type vehicle known as a diti wagon in Nam, and managed to convey to the driver he wanted to find a hotel. The driver drove him to what Raab figured was the center of town. There were several older hotels located there. He checked into what looked like the cleanest one, where the clerk also spoke pretty good English. He left his duffel bag in the room and set off to find a good restaurant.

A short while later he found himself in a dry, air conditioned and rather large Thai restaurant that the hotel clerk had recommended. After ordering a meal and getting his requisite Coke, he looked around at his surroundings. As with everything he had viewed on this day, the interior was ornate. There was lots of color and carvings. He was sure there was a lot of symbolism in them, but he had no one to explain their meanings. He had just started to eat his fragrant dish when a Western couple entered the restaurant. He made eye contact with them and they walked over, taking a table next to his.

"Are you an American?" a middle aged man asked him in a heavy British accent. He seemed surprised to see Raab.

"Yes, sir," Raab said, standing up and offering his hand to the man, who shook it. He nodded to the woman, who remained seated.

"We don't see too many young Americans up here," the man said. "I assume you are a soldier."

"Yes. John Raab, sir."

"Well I am Albert Wilson and this is my wife, Anne. But please sit down and finish your meal, young man."

Raab felt more like talking than eating, but he sat down and picked at his food as the Wilsons scanned the menu. After ordering, they once again turned their attention back to him.

"So, John you're a long way from the party lights of Bangkok," Mr. Wilson said. "How did you find this place?"

Raab explained how he had learned about Chiang Mai and his interest in the Buddhists and their temples. After further questioning ,he spoke briefly about Vietnam and his duties there. Mr. Wilson explained he and his wife owned an export business and that their primary export to England were umbrellas . It made sense to Raab considering all the rain. The Wilson's both spoke fluent Thai and offered suggestions for the best places to visit.

"I was hoping to actually spend some time within a temple, a retreat I guess. I hear they are very peaceful," Raab said. "I need to get back into my own head, if that makes any sense. I only have a week to be here. I realize that it's not much time."

"Well I guess it makes sense, John, if it's important to you. Just highly unusual I say, don't you, dear?" Mr. Wilson said, looking over at his wife sipping her tea.

"I would say unusual yes, but also highly understandable with what I've read about that war," she replied.

Mr. Wilson sat back in his chair and seemed to ponder his wife's answer and Raab's request.

"I guess you need to understand, John, that Thai culture and Buddhism are intrinsically rooted together," he said. "It's not like religion in the States, you know. It is taken very seriously. Lots of symbolism that is hard for Westerners to grasp. They don't believe in God as Christians do. However, they do believe in a soul that is trapped in a cycle of reincarnation -- a continual rebirth of your spirit. It is fascinating to study. I think your problem will be to get someone to take you in for the short time you can be here. I think a good starting point might be the Wat Chiang Man temple. I know some of the monks speak English there. You'll need that so you can understand the instruction they give you."

"My guide today at the Dokmai Gardens mentioned that temple and another one," Raab said. "It sounds like the right place to start I guess. Can you tell me how to get there?"

The Wilsons drew a map on a napkin as they talked about the country and its traditions. It was late when they parted company and he made his way back to the hotel. He fell asleep listening to the heavy rain crash on the tiles of the roof. Tonight it was soothing, not like in the jungle.

CHAPTER 38

The monk watched with interest as the young Western man moved slowly around the temple viewing the ancient artwork and carvings. He could tell the man was not in a hurry and seemed to be praying softly to himself. The monk, whose name was Chah, was a Ajaan or teacher. He sensed something in this man. It was a goodness, he decided. It was so unusual to see such a young Westerner this far from Bangkok. Why was he here? It was disturbing his own meditation. What did this man seek? Could Buddha himself put this man in his path? A strong feeling came over the monk. He must help this man.

Raab watched as the older monk approached him. As the monk stopped in front of him, Raab bowed slightly in respect. The monk smiled and bowed in return.

"Do you speak English, my son?"

"Yes, sir. I am an American. My name is John Raab."

The monk nodded and seemed to carefully choose his next words.

"Why do you come to us?"

Raab had been thinking about this very question all morning and for that matter since he arrived in Thailand.

"I am a soldier and I seek peace for my heart and soul. "

"Perhaps I can help you," the monk replied. "I am Chah. Many people come to us for the same thing as you. We welcome all. You do need not be a Buddhist to seek spirituality. You only need to follow our traditions while you are here."

"I would be honored to do so, Chah."

Chah lead Raab into the temple and pointed out various architecture and statues as they walked. Raab was amazed at his command of the English language.

"We will provide you with a small room for sleep and meditation. Also while you are here I would ask you to wear our traditional clothing as another symbol of leaving your world for now."

A young boy appeared as if on cue. Chah said something to him in Thai and the boy ran off. The two men entered another courtyard and Chah motioned to Raab to sit on the ground. Chah sat across from him, his feet tucked beneath his legs.

"There is no easy answer to what troubles you, John," he said, speaking again in English. "A war is a terrible thing. It robs the soul of peace and contentment. I sense a strong spirit within you that is at odds with where you now find yourself. It is another war that is taking place inside your being."

The monk was silent for some time after that. He was allowing Raab to meditate on what he had said. Raab flashed back to his Jesuit teachers at Loyola. They also wanted you to think about your own feelings and how they might serve yourself and God. He had only been here a short time, but already he felt at ease. The young boy returned and handed him a small pile of clothing. Raab found a white shawl, light blue cotton pants that looked like pajamas and a pair of flip-flop type sandals. A small bath towel completed the ensemble.

"We do not eat again until the morning, but if you are hungry I could provide you with some fruit and tea," Chah said.

"I would like the tea, but I can go without food until tomorrow, Chah."

Again the monk said something to the boy and again he disappeared into another building.

"Come, John, I will show you your room and you can change your clothing. I will then explain some of our teachings so you may meditate upon them."

The room was the size of the prison cell his brother spent his days in. There was a simple bed, a stand with a wash basin and water pitcher on it. Raab removed his clothing, except for his T-shirt and underwear. He had trouble securing the shawl around his shoulders, but finally got it to work. He sat on the small bed and waited for what must come next.

"To understand our teachings, you first must understand the Four Noble Truths," Chah told him after they had seated themselves across from one in a meditation room. Raab was having second thoughts on not accepting the fruit he had been offered earlier. The hot tea had not filled his stomach at all. He normally didn't need much food. His real addiction was for Coke and sweets, especially cake. At the moment he could get neither out of his mind. He tried to focus on the voice of his teacher.

"Our first truth is that there is suffering," said Chah. "It is how I have found you, John. I sense great suffering in your heart. You must first understand that it is there, and you must confront it. This will lead to our second truth and that is the suffering is impermanent and will someday leave you. The suffering is created by ourselves and can only be brought to an end through practicing of "dhamma" or, as you would say, Buddhist life. Those are the last two truths of our simple faith."

"My belief, Chah, is in the Christ," Raab replied. "He is my savior. However I wish to learn from you and understand your religion. I am suffering, you are right. As I said, I seek peace in my heart. I am not sure that I created my suffering -- maybe."

Chah nodded, a serene peace seemed reflected in his face.

"I leave you now, John, for your own meditation of what we have discussed. We will rise early and have our meal for the day. We do not eat after the noon hour. Please remember that this is your own private trip. I am but a guide for you."

As Chad rose to leave, Raab followed him outside and watched as he walked silently away into the night and disappear into the shadows. The moon tried to peek through the almost consistent cloud cover. It had at least stopped raining for the moment. He made his way back to the small room that was now home. He found some books about Buddhism had been left on his small table. A candle had been lit. He looked over the books, all of which were written in English. He found that, unlike Christianity, Buddhism didn't focus on a supreme God. Its precepts emphasized living the present moment and obeying a set of rules similar to the Ten Commandments. There was no set church time. Private worship at the temple was set by the worshipper. Raab chuckled, wondering how that might look in a Catholic church. Not much chance of that ever happening, he thought. He read late into the night before finally falling asleep.

Raab ate in silence with the other monks in the morning. He was struck by the serenity and peace that they seemed to share. He had always been an observer of his fellow man. These holy men were definitely different from other religious groups he had seen.

After their dismissal, Chah once again led him to the courtyard and gardens that surrounded them.

"Today, John, I would like you to meditate on the first noble truth. Do you recall what that was?"

"I do. It is that there is suffering.'"

"Yes, that is correct. We call it "dukkha" and believe that meditation only makes sense when used in maintaining the precepts. It goes to your spiritual core. You must first understand your own suffering. You must ask yourself why the light of life has faded from your eyes. You suffer deeply, John."

Raab nodded. The monk was right. He needed to get his head back on straight.

"Please wander the temple grounds, nothing is off limits to you," Chah said. "We will speak later after you have a chance to look inside yourself. Remember to clear your mind of thoughts that are not necessary."

Chah left Raab sitting near a garden where the novice monks worked to raise crops. He watched them for some time as they tilled the earth. As he did, he began to think about suffering. It was not his own that came to mind. He thought of all the men who had died or were wounded on Hill 875. He could still hear their screams of pain and terror. He thought of his good friend Mike Petrov and his suffering. He thought of Vietnam and the suffering of its people on both sides of the war. Lastly he even thought of his enemies. The NVA and VC. They had no R&R to rehab themselves. They were still out there in the jungle -- suffering. He prayed silently to God and asked him to bless all who suffered. He thanked him for his role as a healer and not a killer. "Let me live a life of peace and justice if I survive this, Lord," he said. By the end of the day, his heart felt lighter.

Raab spent the next two days with Chah, learning from him. He could not remember ever being able to fully explore his inner being so completely. Thoughts of the war didn't dominate his thinking for a change. He even allowed himself to imagine life after the Army. This simple religious life had many appeals, he thought, as he folded the clothing he had worn while here. It was time to return to whatever destiny lay ahead of him. Chah walked with him to the temple entrance.

"I wish we had more time together, John. Our goal can only be enlightenment. It is a path that has its foundation based on generosity and virtue. You are a man who is free from the delusions of the world. You will find a life based faith. Of that I am sure. Go and find your own salvation."

Chah embraced Raab. Both men smiled at each other, then parted. On the train ride back to Bangkok, Raab thought of maybe one day returning here. He had no thoughts of becoming a Buddhist, in fact this experience had him grateful for the religious study he had pursued while at Loyola. It allowed him to see the merits of various faiths and their common goal of salvation. Buddhism had opened up one more door for him. He silently thanked God for the opportunity.

CHAPTER 39

"This is the end, beautiful friend the end, my only friend the end"
"The End," by Jim Morrison

After three days of intense searching, the recon patrol had found no sign of the enemy. SP/5 Taylor had volunteered for the patrol. Just a week before he had been assigned a new medic. His name was Jason Robertson and he was only 19 and fresh out of airborne and medical training. Tyler had been reluctant to send him on a mission, but he was short of medics. He usually had the new guys work at the aid station for a few weeks. During that time the veterans would give them tips on staying alive. Robertson didn't get those benefits. Tyler had reasoned that the mission wasn't too dangerous. The new guy was assigned to a group of soldiers guarding a road. They weren't even in the jungle.

That night VC sappers infiltrated the compound and managed to blow up two of the bunkers there. Several men were injured, including several in the bunker with Robertson. For some unknown reason he left the injured men and started crawling towards the second bunker. Somebody had been yelling for a medic, but it turned out no one was seriously wounded there. He was crawling toward it when a VC soldier ran up and shot him in the head. He never even looked up, Tyler was told by one of the soldiers who witnessed the killing.

So Tyler was having a hard time sending anyone out on missions. He was the medical squad leader and it was his decision that had killed Robertson. The man just wasn't ready, he told himself. The captain had removed him from his duties with the Civil Affairs Team after his return from R&R. He wanted Tyler to devote his time to training the new medics who were arriving daily, replacing a lot of seasoned veterans who were going home. The guys who were rotating out didn't want to go out, and the new guys weren't ready. Tyler resolved the dilemma by taking the missions himself. He remembered when he first got into country, one of the medics in his company had gone out for a new guy who was scared to death. The medic was due to go home in a couple weeks. That night a VC rocket exploded, killing several soldiers. The medic wasn't killed, but he was burned horribly. One of the sergeants saw him in the evac hospital and told Tyler the medic's face looked like a swollen balloon, the burning and edema were so severe. It went along with folklore of Vietnam: You either got it when you first arrived or just as you were going home. Tyler shuddered and was thankful this mission didn't find the enemy. He had too much to live for now. Maggie wrote him daily. Whenever the mail arrived he would have at least a half dozen letters that he would arrange by their postmarks to get them in order. He would then savor every word she wrote. She told him about her return to school. She assured him of her love and their life together someday. She was so excited about coming to California after he got back home. He was hoping there would be mail from her as he headed for the aid station after stepping off the Huey after returning to Ban Me Thuot.

Tyler entered the large tent that served as both an aid station and barracks for the medics of the 2/503rd. As he entered the tent a very intense soldier had a M16 aimed directly at his chest. Sitting next to the soldier was another one who looked very scared, and next to him sat

John Raab, a huge grin on his face. Raab reached over and pushed the barrel of the M16 down. The soldier holding it screamed at Tyler.

"You're not killing me like you did all the others!" he said in a deep Southern accent, looking very pissed off.

Tyler wasn't scared, just confused. Why was Raab here and why was he laughing?

"I was just kidding, Brooks. It was a joke." Raab couldn't quit laughing as he took the rifle from the now confused soldier, stood up and walked over to Tyler, embracing him.

Tyler held onto Raab pushing him out at arm's length and looking into the eyes of his old friend.

"What in the hell is going on, John? What are you doing here and who's that guy?

Tyler motioned towards Brooks with his head.

"Well Brooks here and the guy next to him, Collins, are two of your new medics. Fresh from the old US of A."

Collins spoke up then. "Raab said you didn't like FNGs, you know, fucking new guys, and you usually managed to get them killed right away."

Tyler gave a serious look at Raab. It was one of his horrible jokes and he would have had no knowledge of Robertson's recent death. It was just too close to the truth for Tyler. Raab just thought it was funny, nothing else.

"We need to talk," he said finally. "What are you doing here?"

"Well while you were out looking for Mr. Charles, they moved our whole company here," Raab said. "The rumor is some type of big campaign, but anybody who knows what's going on isn't talking about it."

"Jesus, Raab, it's really good to see you!"

Tyler was genuinely pleased to see his friend. After he explained he wasn't going to do anything to get them killed, the two new medics looked relived. Brooks was from Mississippi and Collins from Maine. He left them to unpack their duffel bags and he and Raab went to the mess tent to scrounge whatever food and drink they could find.

"So I see from the letter you last sent that you're in love, huh Tyler? Tell me about her."

Tyler spent the next hour sipping coffee and telling his friend about Australia and Maggie. His tongue was tired when he finally stopped talking.

"Listen, John, if anything happens to me, you need to let her know. Promise me that you will do that, okay?" Tyler said, looking intently into his friend's eyes.

"Nothing is going to happen to you, Tyler. But just in case, you know I'll honor any request you might make of me."

"Thanks, John, I'll get you her address. It will make me feel better to know somebody besides my folks will know about her. And you know, just in case," Tyler said, his voice trailing off.

Both men shared what they knew about Petrov and what appeared to be his release from active duty.

"Can you imagine him in an Army hospital. He probably pissed everyone off. No wonder they let him out," Raab said, laughing. Tyler was glad he was seeing the old Raab again.

"So tell me about Bangkok," he said. "Run into any hot girls there? Something must have changed your attitude. Your last couple of letters sounded like you were a little depressed."

Raab knew that Tyler would never understand that he was on a retreat, particularly at a Buddhist temple -- no drinking or women. He would think he was crazy.

"Let's just say it was interesting, Tyler. A couple good night's sleep didn't hurt either. I stayed away from the hot girls however. I think the Bangkok whores carry a lot to the same diseases as the stuff we treat here. I can do without that problem."

Tyler nodded, thinking that his friend probably spent his days sightseeing. I've got to teach this guy to surf when we get home, he thought.

Tyler got up to get more coffee and ran into a cook he knew. The captain had told him if he ran short on medics, he could use the cooks to carry supplies on missions. The cooks were aware of this and busted their butts to stay on his good side. The last thing any of them wanted to see was the jungle.

"Listen, Mac, an old friend of mine from the 4/503rd just got here. He has this huge sweet tooth and loves cake. Can you help me with that?"

"No problem, Tyler," the cook replied eagerly. "Just give me a little time brother."

Later that night Raab ate an entire chocolate cake for dinner. Tyler was even able to find some Cokes to go along with the cake. Tyler drank Jim Beam with beer chasers until he fell asleep. All in all it had been a good day.

CHAPTER 40

For the next two days there was no word on the mission or why Raab's company had joined them. It gave Raab and Tyler time to catch up on life.

"I really think Maggie could be the one for me, John," Tyler said. "I am trying to be realistic about our chance of being together down the road. I know I need to finish school first. I can't decide if I want to try playing football again. Maybe I need to consider a smaller school environment. USC might not be an option again. Jesus, I have too many issues on the table."

Tyler sighed as he thought about his future. Raab smiled. It was one of the first times he hadn't heard Tyler lament about his former girlfriend Patty. He might be finally over her, he thought.

"I know the feeling," Raab said. "I don't have a clue of what I want to do if I ever survive this place. I thought about going back to school too, maybe getting my masters and teaching. I just don't know now."

That afternoon, Tyler walked his new medics through sick call for the troops. They treated the usual problems -- colds, sore muscles, jungle rot and one possible case of malaria. He sent that soldier on to the

battalion surgeon for further diagnosis. Then he stopped by headquarters
to see if there was any further info on what was happening in terms of
an operation. If anyone knew anything, again they weren't saying. He
did manage to arrive there just as the mail was coming in. Back at his
tent he was excited to find several letters from Maggie, his parents and
Tim Rowe. After reading the letters from Maggie, he opened Tim's.

Dear Tyler,

*I have trouble believing I am getting ready to finish my junior year
of college. I've been playing a lot of baseball while trying to study
for finals. As usual my folks are pushing for good grades so I can get
into law school. Anyway we are playing Harvard this week and
everyone is up for the game. I am missing spring football again,
which always bums out Coach Boraso, our football coach. It's not
like football is the biggest thing here at Yale. For that matter, no
sports are, not like it's USC or Notre Dame.*

*My dad wants me to work again with him at his office this
summer. Chris has been helping him since she entered law school.
By the way, I think she still writes your buddy Raab. She won't
admit it to me, but I think she liked him. They just didn't have
enough time together. Do you ever see Raab over there? I thought
you said you had been split up. Anyway I really liked him.*

*I also enjoyed all the stuff about Australia, Maggie and surfing.
I haven't been in the water since last summer. Not too much surfing
here in New Haven. When you get home, we'll get back with it.
Maybe I'll go to Australia with you. You just need to be safe and
know that I and a lot of people are thinking of you.*

Your bud,
Tim

Tyler folded the letter and placed it in his foot locker. He had saved
every letter he had received since arriving in Nam. Someday he would
reread them all, he thought. After reading the letter from his mom, he

reread Maggie's letters again before storing them all. He decided to find Raab and see if he had learned anything about the mission. He was starting to get nervous about it for some reason.

"Hey, I got a letter from Rowe," he said. "He said Chris was kind of hot on you still."

Raab laughed. "Fat chance for someone like me with that girl. Too much class and money. She does still write once in awhile and I kind of wonder why."

Tyler had found his friend just emerging from a briefing with his captain. They made their way back to Tyler's tent. Tyler pulled out a beer from the cold medicine case for himself. Raab had a warm Coke.

"So where do you think we're going?" Tyler asked, a little anxiety apparent in his voice.

"Captain said we're headed to the coast, a place called Phu Cat," Raab said. "There's an Air Force base there and a bunch of NVA according to intelligence. It's going to be a joint operation with the South Koreans who are based there and your armor buddies here."

Tyler was glad to hear that the 69th Armor would be with them. The NVA didn't like tanks and he couldn't blame them after seeing what they could do during the Tet offensive.

"I guess we'll get briefed on the helicopter pad on our way out," Tyler said, directing his sarcasm toward his unit's new captain. He had met Raab's captain before and really liked him.

It wasn't an hour later that he was summoned to a briefing on the mission. He was told the same information that Raab had provided. He did learn one additional fact: The operation was to be called "Friendship".

That was great he thought. It sounds like we're all going to Disneyland together.

CHAPTER 41

The information on the NVA's position near Phu Cat had come from a defector named Sergeant Nugen Hong. He had surrendered to the elements of the South Korean Tiger division. The NVA usually avoided the Republic of Korean soldiers, or ROKS for short, who had a reputation as being a fierce fighting force. The Koreans had used their recon units to locate the positions of the dug-in NVA with the help of Hong. When it was determined that the NVA force was of brigade size, the Koreans had requested assistance from their American allies. The American commanders had responded with armor and airborne infantry as well as artillery and air strikes.

The two companies from the 173rd Airborne had dug in with the Tiger Division soldiers and watched as the air and artillery units dropped massive amounts of firepower on the suspected NVA positions. After the strikes, the plan was for the armor to enter the jungle compound followed by the infantry. The captain described it as a "mop up" mission. The paratroopers weren't so sure of that.

It was late in the day when they started to move into the jungle from their fortified positions. The tanks were having a hard time making progress through the thick jungle, but so far the soldiers hadn't made any contact with the enemy. Tyler was lying prone in the jungle grass watching as a one of the Korean soldiers, moving alongside one of the tanks, suddenly stopped in his tracks. He motioned to one of the other ROKS who ran over with a flame thrower. To Tyler it looked like something he had seen in the old World War II movies. American's didn't carry anything that looked like that, as far as he knew. The first Korean lifted a camouflaged ground cover and the soldier with the flame thrower lit a fifteen foot flame down into the entrance of the underground passage. Tyler shuddered. He hated the thought of being burned. He couldn't see from his position if any of the NVA were down there. Sergeant McGuire from second platoon crawled up next to him.

"Hey, Doc, HQ wanted us to pass the word that those spider holes are all over the place so watch where you step in there."

McGuire started to say something else when the sound of the tanks firing ahead of them overwhelmed the sound of his voice. Something was happening. The Koreans were ahead of them with the armor and were also blocking any NVA escape, somewhere north of their position. Raab's company was on their flank. Tyler was next to the RDO and the captain who had not quit talking on the radio since they had taken to the ground, waiting for further orders. He could hear the captain saying "roger that' several times before he finally handed the radio back to the RDO.

"OK we're moving up with the Koreans. They're taking fire and have some men down." He was looking directly at Tyler.

"They need some help, Doc," he said. "The 4/503rd is sending up some of their medics to help too. The tanks are trying to provide cover fire. They'll be in front of you."

Tyler said nothing as he and Brooks, the new medic from Mississippi, moved out ahead of the company. The firefight was intense just ahead of them in the jungle. It appeared that the NVA had managed to set up some sort of ambush. The thickness of the jungle would mean no medevac could safely land there, and Tyler knew any evacuation would need to be back at the clearing he just left. As the men got closer to the firefight, Tyler was constantly looking for spider holes. He didn't want to run past one and have some NVA come out and shoot him in the back.

He followed the trail of one of the tanks that had pushed its way into the dense jungle. This was no place for a tank he thought. He could just see the tank he was following about 25 yards ahead. The crew was firing rounds from their cannon and into the jungle canopy ahead of them. He could see a man down just behind them. He was still moving, but was pinned down by the firefight that had erupted all around him. He could feel his heart hammering in his chest. He could see the ROKS moving out to the flank, away from where the 4/503rd was suppose to be. He and Brooks started to move slowly toward the wounded ROK when he heard the distinctive sound of an incoming mortar. He pulled Brooks down with him as the mortar exploded just to the right.

"Let's go," Tyler yelled to Brooks as he scrambled to his feet and started running before the enemy could adjust their fire. They reached the wounded ROK and found he had multiple shrapnel wounds. The worst was a large perforated stomach wound. Tyler immediately used a compress to hold in the man's intestines, which were spilling out. Brooks was trying to stop the bleeding from a head wound. The sound of small arms fire was all around them, but the tank in front of them offered protection from the most intense of it. They managed to stop most of the bleeding, while the tough little ROK nodded and smiled at them. Tyler started an IV and administered a shot of morphine. He was just going to send Brooks back for a stretcher when Raab appeared out of nowhere carrying one.

"Hey, Tyler, I heard you needed a little help up here," he said, a big grin on his face. His face was dirty and soaked with sweat, but Tyler thought he had never seen such a beautiful sight.

They managed to get the ROK on the stretcher. The fighting had become more intense and the other paratroopers were moving up on their position. Tyler watched as one of them was hit and went down.

He told Brooks to help the man, as he and Raab attempted to carry the injured ROK back to the clearing where he could call in a medevac. They followed the same path back out of the jungle. Another mortar round forced them to the ground once, knocking the wounded soldier off the stretcher. After replacing him, they were able to make their way back to the evac point. They left him with Collins, Tyler's other new medic. He would have to wait for the dust off while Raab and Tyler made their way back into the jungle.

As they made their way back up the tank path, which Tyler now thought was the safest way, he questioned his friend.

"Where the hell did you come from and how did you find us?"

"We were only about 150 yards off to your right. I just followed in behind the tanks until I saw someone. It turned out to be you. Captain said some medics needed help and somehow I knew it would be you."

"Well I for one am very glad to see you. Now just keep your head down."

"You too, buddy."

Tyler caught up with the rest of the company and learned from the captain that the ROKS and armor company had walked into a "Horseshoe" ambush.

"The gooks are in the front and on our sides up ahead. They are dug in and have snipers in the trees. We're going to push forward and the 4/503rd will hold the right flank then move up as we pass their position. Other than the left flank, we have them surrounded."

Raab decided it probably wasn't a good time to try and get back with his unit. There was plenty of wounded here to work on. As they moved up back into the fight, he and Tyler worked together on a variety of wounded paratroopers and ROK soldiers. Now that they had help from the grunts, who were more than happy to take the wounded back to the evac point, the two medics only needed to concentrate on treating the wounded. The battle was still intense in front of their position where the tanks continued to pound the enemy with intense firepower. They were treating a wounded infantryman when a large explosion rocked the ground. It was different from the tank fire. A short time later the RDO ran up to them.

"The gooks just took out the tanker's medical track," he screamed. "All their medics have been killed or wounded. Captain says you need to get up there."

Tyler gave a grim look at Raab. "I know all of those guys, John."

They finished treating the soldier they had been working on and started to move up to help their brother medics. Tyler knew the smaller medical APCs were much more susceptible to rockets and mortars than the tanks they accompanied.

He was right. As he and Raab covered the distance between the paratroopers and the tanks, he could clearly see the medical track on its side. One of the big M-48 tanks had pulled in front of it and was firing ferociously into the jungle with its beehive canon fire in an effort to protect the men who were still inside the track. Raab, who was much faster than Tyler, reached the track first. Inside they found four medics piled together on what had been the side of the track. A quick check found two alive. They pulled the survivors out behind the now destroyed track. As Raab began to treat the wounded medics, Tyler ran to the front of the track to check on the driver. He was dead, so Tyler returned to Raab's position and started to work on one of the downed medics. It was the track commander and Tyler knew his name was Jim. He couldn't remember his last name. His right arm had been almost completely severed. It was barely hanging on, only attached by a couple tendons and shattered bone. Tyler placed a tourniquet above the elbow and tightened it, and gave him two shots or morphine before wrapping the now dead arm in a sling. He knew the best surgeon in the world couldn't save it now.

Another mortar landed in front of the track just as he finished placing a compress on an open wound the soldier also received to his thigh. He and Raab went down, both trying to protect their patients from further damage. The track took the brunt of the explosion and they continued to treat the wounded armor medics. Tyler finished bandaging his patient and after pulling out the stretchers from inside the track, turned his attention to helping Raab. His patient's heart had stopped and Raab was giving him CPR. "Tyler I am losing him. Let's try epinephrine ."

CHAPTER 42

Danh Nguyen Lam slowly lifted the concealed cover of the underground spider hole he hid in. He had been its sole inhabitant for almost two days. He had no idea where his fellow soldiers were or if he would ever rejoin them. He had been a high student in Hanoi only a year ago when his district conscription group told him he was needed for the war effort against the Americans and South Vietnamese traitors. When he entered the People's Army of Vietnam he received only two weeks training before being assigned to a replacement group heading to the south. Many had died along the Ho Chi Minh Trail either from disease or the constant bombings from the American planes. They were told there would be no returning home until they achieved victory. This fight now with the Koreans and the Americans could not be won he realized. Their force was outnumbered and their weapons were no match against the overwhelming power of the Americans tanks. He would never see his home or family again he thought. He would at least die with honor.

The Korean infantry soldiers had found many of their tunnels, but had overlooked his hole. After they had passed by him, going further into the jungle with the American tanks, he had fired his one remaining rocket propelled grenade at the American track that followed the tanks. His aim was true.

He now looked out at American soldiers who were treating the wounded men at the destroyed track. They must be the medics his superiors had told them about.

"These men must be high priority targets for us. When the Americans see their dead doctors, it gives them great fear for their own safety. It is a psychological advantage for the People's Army." Lam remembered his Captain's exact words. What the Captain didn't say was that medical care for their soldiers was scarce. His fellow soldiers rarely received treatment. Many were just left to die alone. He watched the American medics as they knelt over the prone soldier. One was bringing in a stretcher. They will be moving him back towards me soon, he thought. I will be ready.

CHAPTER 43

Tyler dug through his medical bag trying to find the drug and a large hypodermic needle, long enough to penetrate into the heart. He found both and tried to keep from shaking while he prepared the injection. He had never administered a shot to the heart and shook as he stabbed the needle into the man's chest. The drug worked almost immediately and Raab confirmed a pulse. They then got two IVs going and placed the two medics on stretchers for evacuation. The armor units by then had moved further into the jungle and the men from Tyler's unit had moved up alongside of them with the ROKS. Tyler and Raab needed to help carry the stretchers back to the LZ for evacuation. Two of the paratroopers took one of the stretchers as Raab and Tyler carried the medic who had gone into cardiac arrest. Raab was at the front of them as they weaved their way down the same now familiar tank path back towards the clearing. The other soldiers ran in front of them with the other wounded medic. None of the soldiers noticed the NVA soldier who emerged from a spider hole they had crossed more than once. The soldier took aim with his AK-47 and fired several times at the men carrying the stretchers. He watched with satisfaction as one of the men went down, then retreated immediately into his hole.

Raab fell as Tyler released the back of the stretcher. The men in front of him had also gone down. He started to pick up his end of the stretcher when he noticed his friend was down. Raab crawled back to Tyler, who was lying on his stomach. Oh God, no he thought. Not Tyler. Raab turned his friend over and cradled his head in his arms. Blood poured on to his hand from the wound in Tyler's back. Tyler opened his eyes and tried to talk.

"Don't worry Tyler, I've got you." Raab said as he pulled a compress from his pack and applied it to the gaping wound. Raab watched as Tyler closed his eyes.

"Come on man, stay with me." Raab yelled.

Tyler could hear his friend, but he seemed very far away. He was thinking of his parents, about a day they had spent camping in the mountains near Big Bear Lake, when he was a kid. He could smell the pine trees and almost taste the thin, smog free air. He was throwing rocks into a narrow stream that bordered their campsite. His mom was saying something to him, but he couldn't quite make out what it was she was saying. The thought faded and he was now holding Maggie. He was so sorry for her. She had to know how much he loved her. He opened his eyes seeing Raab. He tried to talk, but his mouth was so dry.

Raab leaned in close to his friend's face. It came out in a whisper, but he heard it.

"Tell Maggie ...,"was all Tyler could manage before he died.

EPILOG
SPRING 1972

Tim Rowe had just exited from a meeting with his faculty advisor at the Criminal Justice Clinic. He was helping in the defense of a client charged with a misdemeanor theft. Nothing too exciting, he thought, but it was giving him some practical court experience at the District of Columbia's Superior Court. He was in his third and final year at Georgetown University's Law Center.

He saw him crossing the quad. It was the same lean, sinewy frame walking at a fast pace, his glasses perched on the end of his nose. Tim would have recognized him anywhere, even if he hadn't seen him since the impromptu wake for Tyler, when Raab finally returned from Vietnam in November 1968. He ran after him and caught him before he could enter the library, touching him on the back of his shoulder.

"John, what are you doing here?" Tim said, smiling broadly at his long lost friend.

"Tim, oh my God, how are you?" Raab said. "I'll ask you the same question, what are you doing here?" Raab hugged Tim, pushed him back and just stared for a minute.

"I have a million questions for you. Do you have some time?" Tim asked hopefully. They found a quiet tavern in Georgetown. Tim had a beer, Raab his usual coke.

"I am studying to become a priest Tim, a Jesuit," Raab said after they had settled in at a table.

"A priest?" Tim said. "That's pretty big decision, isn't it?"

"After Vietnam, I was lost," Raab said. "I thought about Tyler's death all the time. You knew I went to Loyola and had a lot of exposure to the Jesuits. I went back and looked up my old advisor there. I was in deep depression. I couldn't get Nam out of my head and all the horror I saw there. He could see the pain in my existence. He suggested a spiritual retreat away from the world, somewhere I could heal and think about my future. That retreat led me to Candidacy which is the informal precursor to becoming a Jesuit. I lived in a Jesuit community for the next year until I entered the Novitiate stage. I decided to become an academic, so I am just starting to work on my master's in theology and one in history. I hope to teach someday, maybe pass on some of the lessons I learned the hard way."

"So when do you become a priest?" Tim asked, leaning across the table to grab some pretzels.

"It will be awhile before I am ordained. It's a long road, Tim. So how about you, what are you doing in Georgetown?"

"I am at the law center. This is my last year. I applied at the FBI and I am going through all the testing and background investigations, as we speak."

"The FBI? I figured after Yale you would find some nice Ivy League law school then join your dad in his firm," Raab said, looking stunned.

Tim looked down at his beer.

"I might not have gone to Vietnam like you, John, but it certainly touched me deeply. When I learned how Tyler died and his sacrifice for his fellow soldiers, I realized that I had never contributed anything to anybody. I almost quit school to enlist in the Army. I saw a counselor at Yale who convinced me there were other ways to contribute to our society and country. You probably won't believe this, but I started going to church. At the end of my senior year I became a Catholic and decided to try and get into Georgetown to study law. I've had my own spiritual journey in many ways since then. Tyler would have loved this. Both of us touched by him in a spiritual sense and the only prayers I ever heard him say were to the surf gods."

"I know God understands love and sacrifice for his people. I like to think Tyler is just fine," Raab said, smiling and reaching over to clink his glass with Tim's.

"Here's to you, Tyler. May God bless you."

A tear ran down Tim's face as he touched his beer mug to Raab' s near empty Coke glass.

"To Tyler."

John R. Hodgson attended high school and college in Southern California. He entered the U.S. Army in 1966 and served in Vietnam in 1967-68. He was a medic in the Central Highlands. He is a retired police chief with the City of Roseburg, Oregon. He has two grown daughters and lives with his wife, Judy, in Huntington Beach, California.

Also by John R. Hodgson, *"Try to Remember"*

To Mike Evasovic and John Maag who were on the journey with me. Our friendship then and now still sustains us.

2.59 million Americans served in the Vietnam War. Of those who served, 58,148 gave their lives.

Tyler is a complex, angry young man who is drafted into the Army after his dismissal from the USC football team and dropping out of college. He has thrown away his first love; his parents are separated, he is in pain and has lost interest in nearly everything. He begins to see his life in a new light after experiencing the horrors of combat. His transformation is almost complete after meeting Maggie in Australia while on R&R. The question for him then; will he survive what waits for him in the jungles of Vietnam after finally finding what he has been seeking?

Tyler and his two friends, John Raab and Mike Petrov go from basic training to medical studies and into the airborne. They come from different backgrounds but form a friendship that is united by the shared experience of war.. They learn how to be soldiers and in the process discover their own inner selves.

ACKNOWLEDGEMENTS

I want to thank Henri Gaboriau M.D. for encouraging me to write this book; Mike Brunker, Senior Editor at MSNBC News, for editing; Donna Mauk for her insight and assistance; and as always Judy for everything.

Manufactured By: RR Donnelley
                     Breinigsville, PA USA
                     July, 2010